IMOGEN BINNIE

NEVADA

TOPSIDE PRESS

NEW YORK

Library of Congress Cataloging-in-Publication Data is available.

ISBN   978-0-9832422-9-1 (hardcover)

ISBN   978-0-9832422-3-9 (paperback)

ISBN   978-1-62729-000-5 (ebook)

10 9 8 7 6 5 4 3 2 1

Cover and interior design by Julie Blair

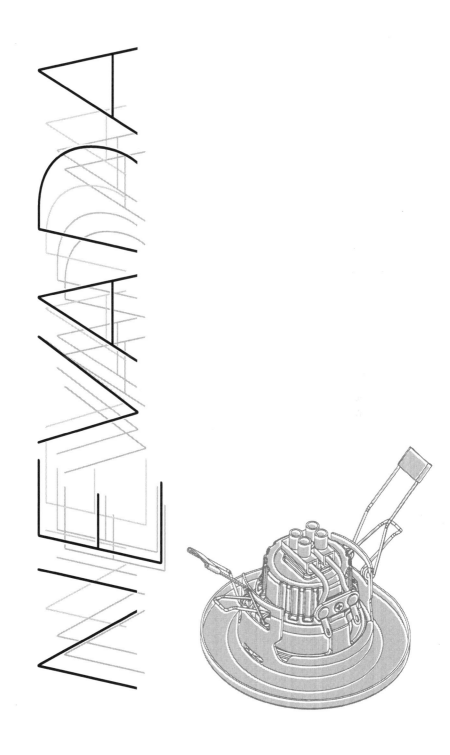

For Pam,
even though it's not a happy book

.

ACKNOWLEDGEMENTS

Thanks to Mom, Dad, Eric and Leslie; to Liam, Aidan, Sylvie, Mark, Jay, Marla, Larry and Phineas; to Julie, Tom, Riley, and Vani at Topside; to Nine, for edits and revision; and especially to Alex, for editing a new revision of this book at least once a year for five years and feeling all messed up every time. Nobody in this book is based on her.

"Sometimes saying goodbye could be so easy
So come on, come on, come on, leave this city"

—Die! Die! Die!, "155"

PART ONE

Late October

She's choking me. She's really in there, fingers on cartilage, mashing my trachea and I can't breathe, Maria thinks. She truly can't breathe, but she can't bring herself to care. There was a time in her life when this was new, when she was at least as hot for being choked as Steph was for choking her, but now they've got an apartment together—a cat, good lighting—and Maria can't even muster a shiver.

She acts like she's into it. She's thrashing, hands at Steph's wrists, pulling. Not that hard, although Steph is probably stronger than Maria, so it's not like Maria could physically make Steph stop if this were for real. And she is turned on. She's pressed up hard on Maria's leg. Then one of her hands is off Maria's throat, at her own crotch, and Steph is getting herself off.

Obviously, there's an art to faking it. Anybody can tell that a parade of porn star squealing and panting is just acting, but convincing somebody who loves you, who you definitely at least used to love, that you're present and choking and hot for it, you kind of have to make yourself believe it. So Maria does.

Her attention is on Steph's fingers at her throat, Steph's substantial hips against her own bony ones, Steph's face.

Now Steph's eyes are closed but you can definitely still fuck this up. You can try to fake it but if you don't convince anybody, nobody gets off, and then you spend the afternoon talking about your relationship. The end part is great, the wine and cuddling and stuff, but the hours of insecurity and tears and feelings leading up to the reconciliation are totally not worth it.

Steph is coming. She doesn't really say anything when she comes, or yell or make noises or anything, but you can feel her shoulders tense and then untense. They tense up really hard. The first time they fucked, Maria was scared that Steph would pull a shoulder muscle.

Then it's Maria's turn. She already knows she's going to fake it. Maria's relationship to her body, it's a mess, she can barely get it together to be naked in front of anybody, much less get off with someone in the room. You'd think it would be impossible to fake it, with junk like Maria's got, but you can. Maria knows some stuff about faking it. One time somebody told her that when she came in their mouth, they could tell she'd come because when that pre-come stuff turned into regular come, it got saltier. But nobody told Steph, because as soon as she's been going down on Maria long enough for an orgasm to be plausible, Maria tenses up her own shoulders for a second and then releases them.

Stupid, yeah. And immature. Maria has told Steph that it's easiest for her to get off from getting head, but the main reason she told Steph that is that when Steph is giving Maria head, she can't tell the embarrassing kinky stories she thinks Maria likes. Which also actually are kind of Maria's fault.

This kind of makes Maria sound like an asshole. This manipulative, lying control freak who needs to be in charge of everything, doesn't have any feelings, hates her girlfriend. But it's just honesty. You fake orgasms because you want your partner to feel like she's doing a good job fucking you, because you feel self-conscious about how closed off from your body you are and how hard it is for you to have a real orgasm. You pretend you're into being choked because she's into it, and besides, four years ago you established a precedent. And it seems like Steph is still into it. Who can tell?

The short version is that Maria feels hopeless about herself and she's trying to protect Steph from that. Maria can't get off with other people. The moment her pants come off, she stops being in her body, and when she's off in the clouds desperately trying to make an emergency peace with her own junk, trying not to think about how bad her junk has fucked up so much of her life and what can she do about it. Plus, Maria likes Steph's junk but on some level she kind of hates Steph for just automatically getting that kind of junk just for free. How do you tell your girlfriend that? How do you make that okay? More specifically, how do you make that okay enough to calm down and get off?

Maria doesn't know, so she fakes it. She collapses, puts on the relieved face. She says, Oh my god, baby.

Steph smiles. Crawls up the bed to put her head in the crook of Maria's shoulder.

You're so fuckin' hot, Steph says.

Hold on, Maria says, trying to give the impression that she's so far gone into the sublime that she can't even talk.

Ha.

2.

Trans women in real life are different from trans women on television. For one thing, when you take away the mystification, misconceptions and mystery, they're at least as boring as everybody else. Oh, neurosis! Oh, trauma! Oh, look at me, my past messed me up and I'm still working through it! Despite the impression you might get from daytime talk shows and dumb movies, there isn't anything particularly interesting there. Although, of course, Maria may be biased.

She wishes other people could understand that without her having to tell them. It's always impossible to know what anyone's assumptions are. People tend to assume that trans women are either drag queens and loads of trashy fun, or else sad, pathetic and deluded pervy straight men, at least, until they save up they money and get their Sex Change Operations, at which point they become just like every other woman. Or something? But Maria is like, Dude, hi. Nobody ever reads me as trans any more. Old straight men hit on me when I'm at work and in all these years of transitioning I haven't even been able to save up for a decent pair of boots.

This is what it's like to be a trans woman: Maria works in an enormous used bookstore in lower Manhattan. It is a terrible place. The owner is this very rich, very mean woman who is perpetually either absent or micromanaging. The managers under her have all been miserable under her for twenty or thirty (or forty or fifty) years, which means they are assholes to Maria and everybody else who works there under them. It's kind of a famous old timey bookstore that's been around forever.

She's been working there for something like six years. People quit all the time, because not everybody can deal with the abuse that comes from this job. Maria, though, is so emotionally closed off and has so much trouble having any feelings at all that she's like, well, it's union, I'm making enough to afford my apartment, and I know how to get away with pretty much anything I want to get away with. I'm not leaving unless they fire me. But when she started working there, she was like, Hello, I'm a dude and my name is the same as the one that's on my birth certificate. Then when she had been working there a year or two, she had this kind of intense and scary realization that for a really long time, as boring and clichéd as this is, but for as long as she could remember, she had felt all fucked up.

So she wrote about it. She laid it out and connected all these dots: the sometimes I want to wear dresses dot, the I am addicted to masturbation dot, the I feel like I have been punched in the stomach when I see an un-self-conscious pretty girl dot, the I cried a lot when I was little and don't think I've cried at all since puberty dot. Lots of other dots. A constellation of dots. The oh man do I get more fucked up than I mean to, every time I start drinking dot. The I might hate sex dot. So she figured out that she was trans, told people she was changing her name, got on hormones, it was very difficult and rewarding and painful.

Whatever. It was a Very Special Episode.

The point is just, there are people at her job who remember when she was supposed to be a boy, who remember when she transitioned, and who might at any point tell any of the new people who come to work with her that she is trans, and then she has to do damage control because, remember, how is she supposed to know what weird ideas these people have about trans women?

Like, what if they are a liberal, and want to show how much compassion they have? 'I have this trans friend' instead of 'Hey trans friend I like you, let's have a three-dimensional human relationship.'

That's what it's like to be a trans woman: never being sure who knows you're trans or what that knowledge would even mean to them. Being on unsure, weird social footing. And it's not even like it matters if somebody knows you're trans. Who cares. You just don't want your hilarious, charming, complicated weirdo self to be erased by ideas people have in their heads that were made up by, like, hack TV writers, or even hackier Internet porn writers. It just sucks having to educate people. Sound familiar? Trans women have the same exact shit that everybody else in the world has who isn't white, het, male, able-bodied or otherwise privileged. It's not glamorous or mysterious. It's boring.

Maria is totally exhausted by it and bored of it, and if you're not, she is sorry. Terribly, appallingly, sarcastically, uselessly and pointlessly sorry.

Maria and Steph get brunch. It's a Sunday morning and they definitely can't afford brunch. Maria has been on hormones for four years but she still flinches at best and dissociates completely at worst if somebody touches her below the waist, and she still has to shave every morning. But still, what's twenty dollars for vegan huevos rancheros and a mimosa?

Steph is in some kind of bad mood. She's nervous about something or sad about something. Maria is trying as hard as she can to pay attention, but she's tired. She can't stay asleep at night. She wakes up grinding her teeth, or worrying about something totally productive like whether she's really a straight girl who should be dating straight boys, or else she just wakes up because there's a cat on her face, purring. Whatever. There are pictures of her from when she was five with bags under her eyes.

There's a waiter on the other side of the restaurant. He's not Maria and Steph's waiter, but he looks familiar. Maria is trying to place him. The only place she might know him from is the bookstore, but it's not clicking.

The tone of Steph's voice changes and she tunes back in. I fucked up, she's saying.

You fucked up, Maria asks back.

I did, Steph says. Do you remember Kieran?

Maria does remember Kieran. Often.

Yes, she says, I remember Kieran.

Remember is kind of a weird word, since he works at the bookstore and Maria sees him most days.

She takes a deep breath, like, I'm just gonna let this all out, and says, I fucked Kieran three nights ago in a broom closet at the gay center.

Three nights ago, Maria repeats.

Yeah, Steph says.

Maria still don't feel anything except maybe little glint in the back of her head that's like, hey, maybe you can break up over this. She doesn't acknowledge it. Instead, she's on autopilot. She can fake it. She's trying to remember what that waiter bought. Was he in history? Art?

She asks, You fucked him three nights ago, but you came home and didn't let on at all for three nights, and you even fucked me this morning without a second thought?

Look, Steph says, but she doesn't say anything else.

Then Maria's brain goes into full shutdown in this way where she's still there, still watching, wishing there were something to say, but really all she can think is, okay, whatever. Maybe Irish history? She thinks, maybe I need to leave. But she can't leave, you can't just bail on your girlfriend in the middle of brunch. She's kind of wishing she were on her bike, about to be hit by a bus, swerving heroically out of the way at the last second. She knows, though, that she's supposed to be thinking about Kieran and Steph in a broom closet.

A broom closet, she says.

Are you okay, Steph asks. You're just being quiet, you're not even making a face.

Maria's brain is shut down because she knows that there

are things she's supposed to be thinking and feeling: betrayal, anger, sadness—but it's like she's just watching herself, thinking, hey, you stupid boy-looking girl, why aren't you having any feelings?

It's a familiar sense of removal that has bothered the hell out of every partner she's ever had. I'm sorry, she always thinks, I learned to police myself pretty fiercely when I was a tiny little baby, internalizing social norms and trying to keep myself safe from them at the same time. I'm pretty astute with the keeping myself safe.

Steph is staring at Maria, Maria is staring at her plate, Steph takes a sip from her mimosa, Maria sips from her own, and then Maria is tearing up, which is new. It's about self-pity, though, not about caring about Steph cheating. She could give a fuck who her girlfriend fucks. It's herself she's sad about. Mopey ol' lonely Maria, the little kid with the bags under her eyes, the lonesome romantic bike fucker, the girl who likes books better than people. It's an easy automatic go-to to characterize things as boring but it is boring to have the same exact things come up whenever anything comes up: poor me. If she were a goth she'd tell you about how broken she is, but since she's an indie-punk DIY book snob, like, here we are.

A tear drips down her nose and then that's it. She wipes her eye near the tear duct, where there isn't any eyeliner, and asks, Okay, so what do we do?

What do you mean, Steph says.

I mean, you boned Kieran, Maria says, enjoying Steph's flinch.

Yeah, Steph says.

Well, do you want to date Kieran? Do you want to be with me? Do we work this out between us?

You're so weird, Steph mutters loudly enough that Maria is probably supposed to hear it.

I'm so weird?

You're so weird! she says again, louder. Are you upset?
I know, oh, you don't have access to your feelings, you're
all shut down, if you were a goth you'd say you're broken—I
know you, Maria, but it still freaks me out, the way you deal
with things.

So you're mad at me, Maria asks.

I am mad at you! I'm sorry I fucked Kieran but it would
be nice if I could get a response to that. It would be nice if
I felt like you cared at all.

Cool, Maria says, You fucked Kieran and you're mad at
me about it.

She lines up five black beans in a row on her fork and
puts them in her mouth. That waiter was definitely in Irish
history. He's sitting at a table across the restaurant, folding
forks and knives into paper napkins.

Steph is crying and Maria is eating. Calm.

4.

Twenty minutes later Steph has probably left but Maria doesn't know because she's gone. She's on her bike. The guy from the Bouncing Souls wrote a song to his bike, and she's singing it to herself, 'I'll sing this song to my bike, and everything else that I like.'

Brooklyn in the fall is another one of her favorite things. Maybe she's already decided that she and Steph are over so she's feeling all free and exhilarated. Or maybe it's just that she's on her bike and it's cold enough to wear a scarf and gloves but not cold enough that you have to wear a heavy coat and a big stupid hat. Either way, she's kind of excited. Brooklyn is gorgeous. Maria is in love with it. When Steph's busy, sometimes she just rides around the whole borough, which is bigger than San Francisco, and explores. There is a zoo, there is a park, there is so much pizza, there is Rocketship in Cobble Hill, there are like four bars where they give you a free pizza with your beer. There are trees and babies and crumbling buildings and there are people.

There's this whole thing now where rich young white people like Maria colonize Brooklyn history because in these messed-up, post-modern times everybody is desperate for something real, and what's realer than the Dodgers and New York Judaism and, like, rap music. The problem is that, when they say 'real people,' what they mean is people who aren't burdened with ironic senses of humor, college educations that help them put up an analytical barrier between themselves and the actual world, and the pressure of living with the reality that they all grew up middle class, chose a broke-ass bohemian life, and now have to deal with the fact that they can't afford the comforts they grew up used to. So they're colonizing those normal people's neighborhoods, colonizing their experiences. It's pretty gross. Maria's aware that she's implicated.

Also, hip-hop is from the Bronx.

You can think about that stuff, or not, while you're dodging buses next to Prospect Park, or nervously cutting through Bed-Stuy, or scoffing at the stupid rich kids in Williamsburg as you stop, chain up your bike, and pay five dollars for a soy latté at a totally independent little coffee shop you just stumbled into.

It's Sunday so Maria has to work. Brunch happened and even though she's got all this seniority, she still doesn't get weekends off. She's off Wednesday and Thursday. On Sunday there really aren't any grownups around, though, so there's a lot of drinking on the clock. Maria feels good about this. She likes drinking, even though she doesn't drink as much as she used to when she was a fucked-up mess of a teenager.

She rides over the Williamsburg Bridge, which is never going to be boring, no matter how jaded she gets. You can see everything in Manhattan. Your legs hurt. There are always pedestrians in the way, and when you get to the bottom it's an opportunity to bust unsafely into traffic, cut between vans and cabs, almost get squashed to death, jump a curb and ride up Third Avenue. Bike messengers probably don't exist anymore now that we have the Internet, but Maria is convinced she would make a good one. She thinks about it a lot.

She chains her bike to a parking meter, punches her card (which is a magnet thing, not a punch-card at all), and drops her giant messenger bag and denim jacket in the employee break room. Her jacket is a work of art. There's a Kids in the Hall skit where Satan gives a stoner the ability to grow weed out of his head in exchange for his perfect denim jacket: that's the kind of denim jacket Maria has. Satan would kill for her jacket. Here are its patches: The Bouncing Souls, White Zombie, the word fuck, a little girl holding giant scissors (on plaid), Hello My Name Is DYKE, and, the coup de grace, the whole back is the cover of the first Poison album. It's not even ironic. Poison rules.

The bookstore only got air conditioning a few years ago, a year or two after she started working here which means half the time when she walks in she's expecting to be pushed back out by a wave of muggy humidity and stink. It was that strong—people used to walk inside in the summer, feel the hot, gross air, turn around and leave. The vibe is still pretty much the same, even if the air itself isn't.

Maria has a specific job, but it's boring, and anyway, she doesn't really do it. Once you've been at a job for a minute, you figure out what you're doing; once you've been there for a few minutes, you master it and can do the minimum necessary without really thinking about it; this is the first time she's been at a job for this long, and she's finding out that she's pushing at the bare minimum, trying to find out where, exactly, lazy ends and We're writing you up begins.

She says hi to a couple people and walks out the side door. She wants a bagel.

5.

When they got together, Maria and Steph were cute as hell. Their relationship started with like two months of Punk Rock Christmas in New York, but honestly, at this point Maria can't even remember it very well. They liked each other a lot. Steph showed Maria about kinky sex; Maria showed Steph about vegetarian cooking. A weird maybe breakup over vegan brunch this morning has Maria going over this in her mind, and reminiscing will always lead to reminiscing hard. On her way to the bagel store Maria is thinking about being a teenager in Pennsylvania.

Firstly, she was supposed to be a boy. She hadn't figured out yet that she wasn't one. She knew something was weird, she had long stringy terrible hair that she wouldn't let anybody cut, the insinuation of an eating disorder, which she certainly wasn't classifying as an eating disorder yet. As far as she could tell, she was a mostly straight boy who just didn't want to eat sometimes with a bottomless belly for drugs. Or at least, an interest in drugs, if not an aptitude. She liked taking drugs, but she wasn't any good at it. She threw up a lot. People in New York take ecstasy or coke in big faux-squalid converted lofts, a dozen stops out on the L or M trains, but where she grew up, they took drugs on the nights they went camping, out in the fields of friends' families' farms. They used to take heroin, too, do lines of it, but nobody in New York seems to. Maybe heroin is kind of nineties. She still misses it though. As far as Maria is concerned, snorting heroin and then lying face down on the floor for forty-five minutes is like the definition of awesome teenage irresponsibility.

As far as she can remember, she never took heroin without throwing up from it.

Anyway, she hadn't figured out she was trans. All she knew about trans people was all anybody knows about trans people before they start looking: that they are all psychos with big hair who trick straight men into having sex with them. On television. Gross. She just knew that she felt weird—but literally every teenager feels weird. Who doesn't feel weird? All the music she listened to was about feeling weird. All the books she read were about feeling weird. So when she was seventeen it didn't seem strange to hang out with, like, a kid who was really into racism and another, a future truck stop mechanic, in a tent, with a ton of flannel and a bottle of Everclear or a dozen hits of acid. In a cow pasture.

That was just, like, what you did. On one level you just went along with what was going on but on another you mythologized what a cool outlier you were and so you internalized a sense of your own weirdness as a badge of pride even as you emotionally dissociated yourself from it. Everybody cool is weird. This is how she mythologized her sense of being trans without understanding that she was trans.

Cow Town, Pennsylvania is a shithole in the middle of nowhere, but it's at the intersection of two roads that'll take you either to New York or the entirely of the West. There's nothing there. Like, there's a downtown, which is really a single block, with a bunch of olde timey shoppes, a five and ten, maybe five hundred antique stores. The crowning glory of Cow Town is a mill that was built in eighteen something that's become a museum. Kids in patch pants sit out in front of the coffee shoppe on main street talking about how they're going to get out, how they're going to start a band or write like Kerouac and go on tour and move to the city. They play hacky sack. It's the kind of place where you'd expect meth, but Maria never really saw much. Sometimes she'd hang out at ye olde downtowne, drink coffee and talk shit too, but especially after this one weird old guy hobbyist stopped selling records out of his living room there, she mostly kicked it facedown in a cornfield. Dude's records sucked anyway. He was a deadhead.

Taking drugs on a farm actually still probably wouldn't feel all that weird to her now, even though she grew tits, but that's just because she carries all that around with her. Who doesn't? All the music we listen to is about carrying the past around with us. All the books we read are about carrying the past around with us. Whatever. She was good enough at school even though it wasn't a priority. The Internet didn't make it out to Cow Town until after high school, so even with her dirtbag friends she felt pretty lonely. There was a Borders an hour away and sometimes somebody would manage to get a zine onto their magazine rack, so she knew that there was more going on than classic rock radio and getting fucked up. She collected strangers' zines. She held onto anything she could find that told her there were things going on outside her own experience: the Church of the Subgenius, Sandman Comics, Maximum Rocknroll, 'alternative rock,' bizarre Canadian sketch comedy.

Eventually she went to college, hibernated drunk for five years, barely graduated, and moved to New York, where the guy in the bagel shop is calling to her.

Yes Miss, he says.

She answers automatically, A toasted onion bagel with sun-dried tomato soy cream cheese, lettuce, tomato, onion, salt and pepper. She's not vegan but she's veganish.

Six years on and it's still weird to be called Miss. Not bad, just like, oh yeah, I guess I did that. Who knows whether that part of being trans ever fades. Probably not. Or more specifically, probably not when you still have to shave, when your junk still gets in the way and makes your clothes fit wrong every morning. It probably doesn't go away until you are rich.

In order not to have to shave every day you have to give lots of money to a professional specialist who sticks electric needles into your face to kill the hair. It's super painful. It's also a lot more expensive to have bottom surgery than every cop show 'Call the paper! The murderer is a *dude*,' plotline might have you believe.

Maria feels resentful about it.

6.

She strolls back into work. Nobody noticed that she was gone, but nobody ever does. She makes a plan. Build a nest by the customer service terminals in the back of the ground floor, eat half of this bagel, help anybody who asks for it, wrap up that bagel, and then go see if any interesting review books have come in. Cool things have probably come out since last time she checked, maybe a week ago. She has so goddamn many books.

So Maria sets up shop at a computer terminal. It is exactly everything everybody complains about when they work retail for the next half hour. People are rude, people are confused, people want her to figure out what they want for them. Whatever. She munches away. This actually doesn't bother her. Maria's retail persona is impressively unbitter. She's watched people burned out on retail be jerks to the public for a long time at this store and it's pretty gross. Plus, this is Manhattan, everyone is an asshole. For a while Maria got into the revolutionary potential of being nice, but now she's kind of over that, too, and gets pretty Zen about it. Mindful. Being a dick to people who aren't being dicks first just leaves her feeling like a dick, which is a shitty feeling. So she's pretty nice.

It is a bookstore, though, so she gets, like, I am looking for this book, it has a blue cover, a lot. It's supposed to be the worst annoying thing you can ask a book seller, but she's into it. People always think they know less than they actually do about a book. She can usually draw it out of them and figure it out. When did you see it? Where did you hear about it? Is it a happy book? These conversations can almost be like a moment of actual human connection, except it's basically a one-direction connection. Maybe in another life Maria will be a therapist or a social worker or something.

In the middle of helping a customer figure out that she is looking for Amy Hempel, who rules, Maria realizes that she doesn't know if she's sleeping at home tonight, or if Steph is, or what. She makes a mental note to call Steph.

All day, though, she keeps forgetting to. By the end of the night, she just wants to go home, but it's not really clear whether she can. Everybody's leaving to get wasted at the bar on St. Mark's with the cheap pitchers, which is always an option, but Maria is exhausted and not really into that idea. She's on the sidewalk outside the closed bookstore and finally taking her phone from her bag when Kieran bumps into her.

My eyes are glaring cunts, he pretty much yells, My cunt a furious eye.

It's a stupid ongoing joke: Kieran heard that Maria liked Kathy Acker so he started doing shitty Kathy Acker impressions at her and normally she responds with shitty impressions of James Joyce, who Kieran is really into. She's supposed to say, Yes I say Maybe Whatever Yes Sure Fine

Yes Whatever Sure, but right now it's not like she even wants to talk to him. It's stupid, anyway. He is supposed to be this End of Gender tough punk genderqueer radical, but it's not like James Joyce was working to undermine patriarchy. Kieran will talk about all the reasons that yes, Joyce was working to undermine patriarchy, but the actual answer was no, James Joyce was a patriarchal fuck and dead white man worship is a function of patriarchy. But fuck that conversation right now. Maria ignores him. Maybe he doesn't know that Steph told Maria they're fucking? She swings her heavy chain-link bike lock around her waist, locks it, climbs onto her bike, and rides into the street. She heads in the direction opposite her house, toward midtown Manhattan.

Obviously you can't ride all night instead of going home, you'll get tired and bored and obviously there is work in the morning, but she decides to ride for a while. One nice thing is that her phone's in her bag, which means if Steph calls she won't hear it. She's kind of aware that she's making herself the bad guy here, that she's kind of acting like an asshole. Whatever yes sure fine yes whatever fine sure who cares.

She rides uptown. Riding a bike in most of Manhattan at night totally rules but riding through midtown is awful twenty-four hours a day. It's practically impossible, unless you are trying to get bruised on a bumper, which is a mood she's in sometimes. A mood she might be in now, actually. Even on a Sunday night like tonight it's pretty gnarly. It's all hills and gridlocked eighteen-wheelers, buses and cabs, so you have to cut between the cars. That's the best, cutting between cars. She pumps her legs up a hill and they start to hurt. She puts a hand out and thumps a taxi's side mirror. This could be the beginning of an all-night odyssey, like Eyes Wide Shut or something, but then she's over a hill, her bike is coasting downhill, and then she's climbing another hill. Her legs protest so she pulls over onto a sidewalk. A movie is actually a really good idea.

It's an exhilarating feeling, when you're so used to not being able to sleep, to decide ahead of time not to sleep. Like, it will feel really bad when you finally get properly exhausted—which will happen unromantically soon—but right now Maria is stoked. She walks her bike two blocks, just off the sidewalk, in the street, so she can self-righteously hog half a lane and get in the way of cars, to a theater where there's a movie playing with a monster in it. She buys a ticket, almost goes in, has the best idea, turns around, finds a bodega, buys a forty, stuffs it in her bag, and goes into the theater.

She can't really drink forties any more. Her twenty-nine year old sad old lady belly can't handle it. But sneaking a beer into the movie is the point, not the actual drinking.

Maria sits in the middle, three rows from the front. There are like two other people in the theater because nobody sees monster movies on Sunday nights. She's been in this theater before. She saw some other stupid movie, with some other stupid monster in it, some other time that she was all emotionally distressed and having, like, a time-out from her normal life. That time the movie had been a matinee and afterward she decided to sneak into a different theater and see a different movie, but then she completely chickened out when she saw a single usher. That stereotype about transsexuals being all wild and criminal and bold and outside the norm and, like, engendering in the townsfolk the courage to break free from the smothering constraints of conformity? That stereotype is about drag queens. Maria is transsexual and she is so meek she might disappear.

She does sneak a forty into the movies, though.

It ends up being kind of a stupid movie, but when we go see monster movies, we are looking for stupid. There are a lot of explosions, the monster is gross, and the plot goes like this: For fifteen minutes, you're introduced to the characters and you think, I fucking hate these yuppies! I wish a monster would kill them.

And then for an hour and fifteen more minutes, the monster takes its time killing them.

It's an annoying, predictable cliché, but Maria always sympathizes with the monster. If you had a conversation with her about it, though, and you implied that there were very obvious reasons, she would flip out on you. This is not the type of insight in which she is interested.

Anyway, it's late, it's like one AM by the time she gets out of the movies. Bars close at four and bookstore people are certainly still drinking, but Maria is starting to feel foreshadowing in her shoulder muscles about what tomorrow is going to feel like if she doesn't get at least a little sleep. So a compromise: she buys a five-dollar bottle of poisonous whiskey at a little hole-in-the-wall liquor store. She sips it on her way home: gloves with cut-off fingertips, riding past the cheap bar on St. Mark's, the permanent traffic clusterfuck at Bowery and Delancy, the Williamsburg Bridge, a navy blue sky without stars and a beer buzz before she even started drinking whiskey.

She doesn't call Steph. She doesn't even check her phone. It's like how if you don't open the official-looking envelope, it can't do anything bad to you. Plus who knows where that phone even is in her bag, plus it's cold, plus right now she's way too busy looking picturesque, like Batman, in this little alcove in the middle of the top of the Williamsburg Bridge, drinking her whiskey and looking at the buildings on the Manhattan side, the Brooklyn side, the Manhattan side. Which is worse? She can't decide.

She likes the metal the bridge is made of, though: these enormous exposed rivets, this net-looking fence so you can't hurl yourself into the river.

It strikes her that she probably kind of hates everything. She picks a fight with herself. Things she doesn't hate: trans women who have just figured out that they are going to need to transition but don't know what to do about it, so they're super nervous but also kind of relieved.

She doesn't hate trans guys who are working on the fact that they've acquired male privilege outside the queer community, but also in a weird way inside the queer community, especially in the way that their presence tends to eclipse or eliminate or invalidate that of trans women, so they're working on it and starting conversations about it and being accountable to trans women.

She doesn't hate puppies.

Pretty much everything on cuteoverload.com is pretty okay, actually.

A hitch in her throat tells her to stop being all romantic and weird and getting trashed, Batman, so she starts riding again, more or less freefalling down the other side of the bridge, thinking about cuteoverload.com. That video where the baby panda sneezes. There are probably other things she doesn't hate.

Feminist theory, she proposes. I guess I don't hate feminist theory.

She doesn't hate having a favorite obscure band that she keeps a secret and doesn't tell anybody about because sharing it would ruin it. That one is kind of nice.

She definitely doesn't hate Piranha, her one trans friend who doesn't drive her up every fucking wall. Fuck, she's owed Piranha a phone call for like three days.

She probably doesn't even hate Steph. Like, as a couple they are fucked, and obviously Maria sucks at changing the things in her life that she really needs to change. Such as: she totally needs to break up with Steph. But for real though, Steph rules. She and Kieran, y'know, that sort of thing just kind of happens sometimes, especially in a queer relationship, right? And it's not like Maria never fucked Kieran while she was with Steph.

She forgot that she was making a list. She takes the little flask out of the bag and lifts it to the light. There's only about a quarter left. She thinks, wow, I am pretty lucid for a forty and 600 milliliters of whiskey, and then she thinks, what was I thinking about? A list? And then she's at the bottom of the bridge, waiting at the weird turny corner light.

Oh, Williamsburg. There was a point when you seemed like a scary, tough neighborhood, but now it's obvious that the graffiti on your walls gets put there by art students.

7

Maria kind of fucked Kieran first. Steph knows about it. It was a pretty big deal when it happened, and Maria has been sporadically remembering, wincing, and trying not to feel like an asshole ever since. What happened was that he started working at the bookstore a little over a year after Maria started injecting estrogen, when people she didn't know were starting to read her as a woman most of the time.

He is trans too. He's pretty into it: for Maria, being trans is like, Here is this shitty thing I have to deal with, but for Kieran it's like, Fuck yeah! Being trans, all right! Trans guys seem to have this relationship to being trans a lot more often than trans women. It's understandable. Sometimes trans guys come out of radical activist dyke communities where having a punk rock gender is kind of like, chic, or whatever. Whereas for trans women, this tends not to be the case. When they come out trans women tend not to have the analysis that comes from having existed in a queer community where people talk about gender; the mistake some people make is assuming that this means trans women never put together an analysis.

There's also a thing about cultural norms about masculinity and femininity that everybody internalizes, and the kind of light that throws on the different directions of transitioning, but whatever. Who cares. It's hard to explain. Maria's been mentally outlining a zine about this stuff that will lay it out clearly and solve everything since, like, before she started transitioning.

So Kieran started working at the bookstore, read Maria as trans, and decided to be her friend. It was great because Steph knows queers but gets anxious, and Maria doesn't talk at parties so neither of them has ever been particularly enmeshed in a queer community, but Kieran was. That fucker knows everybody. You'll be like, Oh, Judith Butler's written a new book, and he'll be like, I threw her over a table and fucked her at brunch once.

You're like, Really?

And he says, No, but I did have her come read at my school when I was in college.

So they became friends, they ate lunch together, it was a new relationship, even though it wasn't supposed to be a make-out relationship. They talked about stuff, he explained stuff to her—he loves to explain stuff—and she was like, oh my god, here is a person who knows the real smart truth about transitioning! Gender truly *is* a construct!

Eventually you can't help but figure out that, while gender is a construct, so is a traffic light, and if you ignore either of them, you get hit by cars. Which, also, are constructs.

They fucked in a Burritoville bathroom.

He managed to kind of fuck her with a packer in a tiny, dirty yellow bathroom downstairs in the Burritoville on Second and Sixth. She managed to keep her skirt on the whole time and not to let him touch her junk. She certainly didn't come. Maybe he did. There were greasy patches on the mirror and since the bathroom was so small she pressed her face against it while he kind of fucked her, and then when they left there was grease all over her cheek. It was hard to wash off. She was like, cool, punk rock, degradation, kinky sex, how queer and great. That was her sleaziest moment. It seemed like, from then on, she'd be a building a body of work about the interesting sex she'd had, but those stories never really materialized. That time at Burritoville, that was pretty much it.

She's thinking, I think I just don't *get* sex, while she shoulders her bike and starts climbing stairs. Maybe one day, when my seven hundred dollars of savings become twenty thousand and I can afford bottom surgery, I'll be able to get past the inevitable shutoff point and actually enjoy it. Can't wait.

She opens the door and the cat isn't in the kitchen, which means she is probably in the bedroom with Steph. Kieran probably isn't here. The cat hates everyone except Maria and Steph.

The cat appears and rubs her little black head on Maria's leg. Hi cat, she says.

She opens the fridge, which is empty, prolonging her own anxiety in a really familiar way. Like, if Kieran were in Maria's bed with her girlfriend, not that Maria owns Steph's sexuality or anything, but it would be pretty stupid for her to be in the kitchen in a scarf, one glove on and one glove off, thinking about a middle-of-the-night stir-fry, while he was in there spooning her. Getting his sweat and come and lube all over Maria's blankets.

Ew.

Steph sleeps pretty deeply, so Maria walks down the hall, all three feet of it because this is a New York City apartment, and cracks the door. She's asleep by herself. Maria goes back to the kitchen, finishes her little bottle of whiskey, accidentally leaves the kitchen light on and the refrigerator door open, and passes out on the couch.

At four or so she wakes up all headachey and sets her phone alarm—Steph had called, kind of a lot of times—turns off the light, closes the fridge and goes back to sleep on the couch in the kitchen. So bohemian.

8.

Maria misses Steph in the morning. Steph has a grownup job so she's up and gone before Maria wakes up, which is funny because usually sunlight, a car horn, her own breathing, anything will wake Maria up. Good work last night, whiskey, too bad you can't make sleep as restful as you make it deep.

Turns out Piranha texted Maria last night, too. Fuck. Mostly her texts are just a bunch of cussing, because Piranha knows that Maria likes cuss words. She's a good friend. But last night she was like, Dude, where are you? Maria texts back: Sorry dude. Hang out soon?

She's exhausted and feels half-dead, but that's really not new. Her alarm leaves her exactly enough time to shave, puts on makeup and get out the door. She rushes: there's a schedule for sleeping as late as you can, if you're economical enough with your time in the morning. She slept in her clothes, which saves her almost four minutes of getting dressed.

She got very cold one night at Camp Trans, the year that she went, and put on all of her clothes: a dress, a long skirt, jeans, a hoodie, that denim jacket. It ended up being kind of a great outfit. Plus jeans and multiple skirts means no stress about, like, anatomy. It basically became her uniform. Like, she'll change her underwear. It's hard to admit but she has exactly one bra that she likes, and a bunch that she hates, so she wears the same bra every day but theoretically you could change your bra too. You just rotate out a dress or put on the other hoodie and voilà, new outfit. Same clothes every day! It's a non-appropriative mantra. She's even gotten good at riding a bike in a long skirt.

Because shaving and putting on a bunch of foundation every day are emotionally exhausting reminders of being trans, she gets a step removed from them by monologuing like she's explaining them to someone. Secret trick one is to boil water in a kettle on the stove while you get dressed and brush your teeth, then stop up the sink and make yourself a little boiling lake. If the water is so hot that it truly hurts your fingers when you splash it on your face and you kind of worry that you're doing permanent damage to your skin, you are doing it right. Super hot water makes the shave closer, who knows why. Maybe like how you have to warm up a tortilla before you can make anything out of it? Anyway then you smear shaving cream all over your face. Use the cheapest stuff you can find: sometimes Barbasol has a kind that says Real Man on the side, that's the best one. Shave your face with one of those triple-blade razors. They're expensive, but you can re-use them for like a couple weeks. You'll know it's time to replace the blade when your face is a gory mess every day after you shave and you keep thinking, you want blood moon magic but you only bleed a couple days a month? I bleed every day.

From my face.

Anything more than three blades is for rich people.

Secret tip number two is to get some of that face lotion stuff that smells like an old lady. After you've shaved and washed off your face, glob it on everywhere and give your face time to suck it in. It makes your skin softer, which helps gross middle-aged businessmen slumming in your store know that you are the one to hit on.

For makeup: Okay. If you still need to shave, you are still going to have a little bit of, like, beard shadow on your face. A lot of people will tell you to slather on tons and tons of foundation, or the trick where you put lipstick all over your head and then cover it in foundation, but they are stupid. The truth is that nobody is going to look at your chin very hard, so all you need is normal foundation you can get at Sephora. The cheapest stuff there. Powder foundation, liquid foundation, who cares. Get it all over your face, your nose, down your throat to past where your fur ends. Sometimes you can get lucky at the drug store, but mostly you just want the cheapest stuff at the fancy store. If everything else is working right, heavy layers of makeup are more of a This Person Is Trans sign than the implication that there's a mustache hibernating under that foundation.

Secret trick number three is to get as much eye makeup on your eyes as you can. People will disagree about this but fuck them. It took years of research but the current theory on the reason this works, and complimentarily why lipstick makes you look all unhinged, is that you are drawing the beholder's eye toward your eyes, away from your beard shadow area. Lipstick draws the eye toward the bottom of your face, where the hibernating stubble lives. Fuck that.

So put lots of black shit around your eyes, like Ally Sheedy in the Breakfast Club. You will look kind of goth. Can you pull off kind of goth? Do you want to? If not, here is secret thing number four: sparkles. Apparently sparkles on a trans woman are kind of a cliché, but this is the thing, the truth that underlies all of this makeup advice: nobody is expecting to see a trans person. Girls are allowed to wear sparkles on their eyes. If you wear lots of sparkles and, like, blood red lipstick, without foundation, and a low-cut shirt that shows off a flat expanse of chest, then yes: people will heckle you and try to intimidate you. But nobody expects trans women to be wearing sparkles, to have a fucked up growing out dye job and tons of dykey punk shit covering every inch of their skin. So.

Maria is tall and thin, though. She's already getting the benefit of the doubt. None of this stuff might work for you.

This ritual takes five minutes from the time the kettle starts whining.

A couple weeks ago Maria bought a four-foot tall rip-off print of Piss Christ, the picture of a crucifix in urine that everybody flipped out about in the early nineties, for fifteen bucks from a weirdo on St. Mark's. She brought it out to Piranha on the train because she thought Piranha would be into it. And she was. She literally teared up when Maria showed up at her door with a huge and awkward framed piece of art. She didn't cry though, she was fine in a second, and then she insisted on giving Maria a bag of pills. Maria was like, okay, that's cool, thanks, while Piranha explained which pills were which. These ones are Percocets, these are morphine, these are Adderall, these are Vicodin, careful with these. Maria's not really even that into drugs any more. Nowadays taking drugs just seems exhausting, four hours of yay and then like three days of ugh. Plus, puking. The worst is the part where you are choking up your guts and you can't breathe, and it seems like more and more, as she gets older, that's all that happens.

Pills are okay. Whatever. Heroin's too down; coke's too up and then too down. Psychedelics just take too long, and then you feel weird for a week. Smoking weed makes you totally stupid, and Maria's already pretty dumb. No, to be more specific, smoking weed makes her useless and unable to do anything, and she's already pretty bad at making herself do anything besides beat herself up for not doing anything.

So once she's put on her face, she takes two Adderall from the crumpled and powdery little sandwich bag with the idea that they'll kick in by the end of her half-hour bike ride to work, and then she'll be super productive all day. Or at least, for the first six hours. One complicating factor is that she's never really sure which pills are which, so these ones she just took are probably Adderall but they might be anything. Hopefully they're not morphine. Morphine is the worst. One morphine is kind of floaty but two morphines are one five-hour stomachache and then three pukings.

Anyway, makeup secret from a trans woman number five: Take pills.

Maria used to have a pretty strong body, back when she was an energetic little college kid who looked like a dude and journaled obsessively about gender in top secret notebooks all day every day. But now she is old, almost thirty, and she's been going sleepless and depressed and drunk for so long that her body starts feeling like it's collapsing at the slightest provocation. Seriously, the sun hurts her eyes, her belly feels like old dry leaves turning wet while they rot, and her shoulders throb from just a forty and a little whiskey, but she's got to be at work. So: Adderall.

Riding into Manhattan takes longer than usual because she usually has a beer or two or a glass of whisky before bed, not a forty and a flask. She gets into work late. Oops. They are probably looking for reasons to fire her, because she's been here so long and she's gotten so many mandatory union raises that she can almost afford food and rent, so being late is kind of a big deal. Like, when you're in the union, they can't just fire you.

She spends the morning waiting for the axe to fall. Like, she's not just going to get flat-out fired, but she might get talked to. They do this thing where they show you a computer printout of your clock-in times. It's just a gross atmosphere. But it's fine! Turns out she was right and it was Adderall that she took, which means she is super focused and gets a ton of work done. She dusts the shit out of a bunch of displays, rearranges them, shelves a million books, helps tiny old ladies find old, tiny books, and barely even sneaks out the side door for extra bonus breaks at all, except a couple times. Around noon she's thinking, I am the MVP of this shit, when she bumps into Kieran, on his way outside for a cigarette.

Dude, he says.

He's wearing an old, worn out and misshapen white t-shirt, suspenders, and baggy corduroy old man pants with a tie loose around his neck. They are clown clothes, but they look frustratingly good on him.

Dude, she says.

Come smoke a cigarette with me?

I quit, she says.

Okay, he says, When's your lunch break?

Jesus, she thinks. He is going to make sure that we have a talk.

I'm going at two, she says, do you want to come with me?

Yeah, he says, I do.

It's nice that she's all rushing on drugs, getting like a buzz from productivity, because she actually does kind of feel like working this out.

She shelves books for a while. Kind of. Mostly she looks through the carts of books to be shelved and mostly she just flips through the stuff by writers she already knows she likes: Dennis Cooper, Robert Gluck, a first edition of a Joe Meno book nobody else seems to have cared about. She keeps getting sucked in and has to force herself not to just lay around reading.

She's furtively flipping through an Ali Smith book and getting kind of sad when Kieran does that thing where he taps her twice on the back of one shoulder but he's standing on the other side, so she spins around the long way looking for him. He is annoying.

Are you ready to go?

Okay, she says.

They clock out, go outside, start walking. She realizes they're walking toward the burrito place where they did that thing. Awkward, she thinks, and then, no, just really bad taste.

Steph said you talked to her, he says.

Kind of, yeah.

She said she told you that she and I are doing it, he says.

Yeah, Maria says. She's not looking at him or inflecting any words.

She said you weren't really talking to her at all about anything and that—

How much have you been talking to my girlfriend, she asks, interrupting him. I didn't even know you all knew each other.

Yeah, he says, It's kind of awkward. He does a little jump step. Maria is still high on Adderall. Where does this guy get all this energy?

Goddam right it's awkward, she mutters.

Hey y'know MySpace? he asks.

Yeah, I know MySpace, she says, You and I are MySpace friends.

There's a beat.

Wait, she says, isn't Facebook the thing now? Isn't MySpace kind of passé?

Nah, MySpace is cool again, he says. Facebook redesigned their thing and it's all weird.

Oh.

Anyway, listen, he says, Steph and I became MySpace friends because I saw her on your top friends, thought she was hot, and totally friended her.

Jesus Christ, really? She's thinking: is this what my life really looks like? Obviously everybody's life looks like this, when little kids have flickr accounts and old men are on match.com and if you're not online anywhere then you are making a statement, but for fuck's sake. He saw her on MySpace? Surreal. Kind of embarrassing for everyone.

Yeah so, he says, but she cuts him off again.

Look, I don't care, she says.

You don't care, he repeats.

Kieran, I took an Adderall this morning before coming to work, and I am coming down from it. I postponed a hangover with it, kind of, although not really, because I have been feeling hyper and shitty all morning. I really don't want to talk to you about the ins and outs of me and Steph and I really don't want to talk to you about the ins and outs of you and Steph. I think probably I should talk to her about this, instead of to you, *mais oui non?*

She said you won't talk to her, he says.

They're outside the restaurant and Kieran stops, but Maria keeps walking. Whatever. Is this a theme in her life now? Poking around the city, going places she doesn't care about and doesn't have time to go to? Obviously on some level she's trying to give herself room to figure out what to do about herself and Steph—but on another level, obviously she's figured out what to do. It's time to leave her. Obviously, right? We've been here before.

The sky is grey in this perfect New York Way and Maria is walking downtown, down Second toward where probably Lower East Side used to be but now it's just a bunch of, like, Subway franchises. And Moby's restaurant. She's thinking about Kieran, sitting in the burrito store, bouncing and munching all unperturbed. That motherfucker does not sit still.

She realizes that she's intentionally trying not to think about Steph, so she tries intentionally to think about her. How she feels about her now, how she used to feel about her. When they met, Steph was this pretty, fat femme who made fun of people affectionately and called people lezzies and faggots as terms of endearment. Now her bright red hair is black. Her bright red clothes have become black. She grew up. Her job exhausts her and her girlfriend exasperates her.

Maria is like, what the fuck does that have to do with me, though? I didn't do anything. Like I guess I got comfortable and when I'm comfortable, all I want to do is read. I get quiet. It's not like she and I go out to bars or anything these days, but it's not like we ever did.

The more she tries to think about it, whittle it down to how she feels about their relationship, the slipperier it gets. Thinking about Steph is like trying to squeeze a fish. She's getting confused and lost and then she's, like, way the hell downtown, in Chinatown, and she really should go back to work. Opportunity number two for an odyssey of city exploration as a metaphor for self-exploration: poof, down the tube. Whatever. She does have this feeling for a moment though of what it would be like not to be tied to Steph, to their apartment, to her job, but then she thinks, that's some straight dude bullshit, the self-sufficient loner. She felt liberated for a second, though.

9.

On the train on the way back she thinks about how she could, actually, just ride uptown, like go to Central Park or something. Her hands are already kind of numb, and all her shit is back at work, but people leave for lunch and don't come back sometimes. A few years ago, Maria worked with this boy who was probably okay, but they would have these intense, fucked up arguments. She'd provoke him with something like, Dude. You don't like Hole? Is it because you are a misogynist?

He'd get all pissed, flip out, and try to explain that he wasn't, in fact, a misogynist, and actually what he liked was hip-hop.

But dude, Maria would say, You already admitted that you don't like Sylvia Plath, and now you think Courtney Love is a shitty guitarist.

Stuff like that. Who knows. The point is, when Maria argues, she gets more and more laid back, especially when the other person is getting loud and flustered. So he'd be getting upset, she'd be poking and poking, and eventually he would whip a copy of The Da Vinci Code at her head and storm out, never to return, at least until tomorrow. All afternoon everybody was like, what the fuck Maria. And like, Man, I wonder if he'll come back today! He didn't.

The next day she'd be like, Sorry, and he'd be like, Yeah, me too, and then they'd never really talk about it again.

She's thinking, I could just do that, but then the train pulls into the station by the bookstore and she gets out. Nice romantic fantasy but she's already about to get written up for tardiness and to be real who knows how possible it is to find a job with a transition in your background. She tries not to think about whether that means she'll be here untill she dies.

10.

Steph is waiting at the bookstore.

Jesus, Maria says. I can't talk to you right now, Steph.

You don't have to talk to me right now, Steph says. I just wanted you to know that I'm staying with a friend, who so you know is not Kieran, for a couple nights. I want you to figure out what you want from Us, whether you want anything from Us.

The Adderall's leaving her head, which has started pounding, and Maria doesn't want to have a loud argument with her girlfriend in the store, even though she's union, so she says fine, whatever, sure. Steph stomps off and Maria is like, thank god. The apartment to myself tonight. I am going to take such a fucking nap.

The rest of the day is brutal, the kind where you're so tired you're past tired, time just drags, and if you can come up with a project to occupy yourself it'll pass but you're too tired to think of a project that doesn't require too much energy? She sneaks out the side door but she doesn't feel like walking around. She hides in the bathroom with an old Rebecca Solnit book, but she keeps falling asleep. She thinks about taking another Adderall but then she wouldn't be able to sleep when she gets home.

The other career path that people have at this store is that they work here for six months or a year and then leave for an entry-level position at Harper Collins, but it's always been clear that that wasn't Maria. She's thinking about that, rearranging books on a cart and not looking at anyone, when a thing falls into place. She's like, everybody I like ends up leaving this shitty job, why do I stick around? She's like, I'm the sort of person who has too much self-regard to stay at this job, too, except I guess I'm all damaged.

Meaning: trans. Not in, like, an I should not have transitioned sense. More like, okay, I have been trans since I was a tiny little baby. Whether it was something in my brain from before I was born, like people argue sometimes, or it was something I picked up developmentally after I was born, like other people argue sometimes, or whether somebody sexually abused me and then I repressed the shit out of it and then that repression transmogrified into transsexuality, as some other folks will argue, who fucking cares. Maybe there is a gene, maybe it'll turn out Freud wasn't a crackpot who liked logic games more than human beings, maybe my mom was overbearing and my father was distant. I don't care, whatever, I'm trans. I have been trans since I was little. There is this dumb thing where trans women feel like we all have to prove that we're totally trans as fuck and there's no doubt in our minds that we're Really, Truly Trans. It comes from the fact that you have to prove that you're trans to psychologists and doctors: the burden is entirely on your own shoulders to prove that you're Really Trans in order to get any treatment at all. Meaning hormones. It is stupid and there are these hoops you have to jump through, boxes you need to check: I have only ever been attracted to men, I have never fetishized women's clothes or done anything remotely kinky, I have never been sexual with the junk I was born with. Pretty much you have to prove that you're totally normal and straight and not queer at all, so that if they let you transition you will be a normal het woman who doesn't freak anybody out, and so we often, as individuals, internalize these things, and then we, as a community, often reinforce them. All of which is relevant specifically because you are supposed to have known you were trans since you were a tiny little baby.

Maria didn't though.

She felt weird when she was little, but she assumed everybody else did too. She didn't figure out what kind of weird until she was like twenty. She'd known something was messed up, that she was distant from everything. She'd known that Those Kinds of People were out there somewhere, but it felt like there was nothing but us normal people in here. This is what everybody thinks. When she was twenty she figured out that she was such a mess not because she was trans, but because being trans is so stigmatized. If you could leave civilization for a year, like live in an abandoned shopping mall out in the desert giving yourself injections of estrogen, working on your voice, figuring out how to dress yourself all over again and meditating eight hours a day on gendered socialization, and then get bottom surgery as a reward, it would be pretty easy to transition.

She's thinking about bottom surgery, wondering if other trans women who have been transitioning or transitioned or whatever for as long as she has still think about this stuff, or whether it's just all up in her face every time on the rare occasion that she takes her pants down so she can't get past it, when Kieran is all bouncing like six inches from her face.

Jesus, Kieran, she says.

Deep in thought, right? he asks.

I guess so.

Do you want to get a beer? I seriously want to talk to you.

No, Maria says, I'm going home.

Gross, he says.

Gross, she says back.

Okay, but I really do want to talk to you, pretty soon, he says.

Okay, she says.

Then her shift is over and she can go home.

11.

What she should do is pick up some vegetables, go home, make a stir-fry, and then munch on that for the rest of the night, either with a notebook or in front of the computer. Relax, but also, instead of watching movies or going on romantic, lonely adventures, stay at home and get centered—lezzie—and figure out exactly what she needs from Steph, where both of them stand in relation to each other. Not get a bottle of wine.

Soon, though, that idea has eroded. A bottle of wine helps you get past your mental inhibitions to figure out how you really feel. It brings down your automatic defenses. There is a Trader Joe's on the way home from work, which is totally weird in New York City, and they probably have cheap not-awful bottles of wine there, but if you developed an arbitrary punk rock system of morals about chain stores when you were sixteen, that's a hard choice to make. She buys one at the corner store on her own block. The corner store is reassuring because it's dusty and feels like Old New York and also because when you go to the corner store you're not putting money into the pocket of Trader Joe's

Hawaiian shorts. Proud of herself, she hauls her bike up the steps, locks it up outside the door, goes inside and pours herself a glass of wine and turns on her computer.

Then she has another glass of wine. Then she's asleep.

She wakes up and looks at the clock. It's ten thirty and she's still exhausted. It occurs to her, half-asleep and bleary, that she might actually sleep through this night. It doesn't occur to her to slap herself awake, put on an album and get to work solving her life. She's so grateful at the possibility of actual REM sleep that she rolls over so no light can diffuse through her eyelids.

12.

She wakes up around four thirty and feels rested. Do other people feel like this all the time? It's fucked up. Her head feels all clear and she thinks for a second about pouring herself a glass of breakfast wine, but then she thinks, no this is perfect! I have four hours until I have to be at work, which means I can shave, put on makeup, then go to Kellogg's and write for two and a half hours. As the sun is coming up, no less.

So she does. Shaving at five AM means she's going to be visibly beardy by like three, which is gonna suck for the last couple hours of work, but it seems like she's only ever visibly beardy to herself. Nobody else ever seems to notice. Nobody ever really gets six inches from your face and scans for stubble though, plus lots of girls have hair on their face, plus it kind of hides behind foundation a little bit, plus gender is totally 100% performative, right? Whatever! All you gotta do is perform Lady, totally embody it, and then nobody will care about anything.

She's getting kind of manic, actually. She's going to be tired early, but that's totally great because maybe then she'll get on a normal sleep schedule, where she's too exhausted to move by eleven o'clock every night, and she wakes up totally stoked every morning at seven. No, five! And solves her life at Kellogg's! Every morning forever!

Then she's tired and bored of being excited. She puts on extra too many sparkles around her eyes out of zealousness. Other people really feel this way regularly?

13.

Kellogg's is a shitty diner right in the middle of Williamsburg. Williamsburg is a weird little neighborhood in Brooklyn, right next to Manhattan, where a ton of artists and queers started living about twenty years ago, when Manhattan started being too expensive. They displaced a bunch of Hasidic Jews, which is gross, especially since now it's all people who look like they're in experimental disco punk bands because they are in experimental disco punk bands. It's pretty creepy.

And Kellogg's actually used to be a shitty diner right in the middle of it, although they redid it a little while ago and now it's way less shitty, even though the onion rings are still greasy, the coffee's still burned and everyone who works there still seems like they hate you. In Maria's trite lifelong quest for authenticity, Kellogg's still kind of rates a blip. The sky is just starting to turn from black to blue as she's chaining up her bike outside.

Bars in New York close at four. What this means is that Barcade, which is across the street and down a little from Kellogg's, kicked the last bunch of drunks out into the street about an hour ago, and since they were drunk they wanted greasy things. So they're all inside Kellogg's at five fifteen on a Tuesday morning. They are probably graphic designers or something? Telecommuting, expensive fake-DIY haircut, drunk graphic designers.

These are the situations where, if you are trans, you are going to get read as trans, and it is going to be a situation. It hasn't happened to Maria in a long time, but it used to, and that sort of experience leaves a mark so she's hoping the little corner booth under the fake tree is empty so she can hide out there with her face in her notebook and the drunks will ignore her.

She goes inside and the place is packed with haircuts and vintage jackets. Whatever, fuck 'em. Maria's aggressive veneer of tough monsterness goes up and she stomps through to the table in the back, which is empty, like she's wading through a river, head down, no reason to stop. Nobody notices her. It's funny. Nobody ever does any more. It's just that when they used to, they were so vocal about it that still, to this day, you worry. Sucks. Whatevs.

You can't help but wonder what people see when they look at you. Androgynous fag? To be real that's a look she tried for when she first started transitioning, which doesn't disrupt strangers' worldviews much and theoretically they will just ignore you. But no, you can tell that Maria has tits, you can see from the cleavage she's sharing with the world that they're not pretend. She wears pretty small tank tops. Maybe they just know what a transsexual is and are respectful?

Yeah. Totally. Clearly.

It's been her experience that if people look at you and figure out that you are trans, they are pretty eager to tell you. No matter their demographic, teenage boys like to talk shit loudly so their friends can get in on it, older women like to wink or give a sly little smile, straight men who know they're boring make angry faces, straight men who think they're cool give you a smirk, straight women will give you a quiet little aside to let you know that they are totally onto you, gay boys want to be your best girlfriend (except the HRC type, who think that you're trying to steal their rights), and dykes.

Dykes are hard to read. Too much expectation and stress.

So the whole time all these people are failing to make all these responses to her, to the fact that she exists, Maria is trying to drink as much coffee as she can. And to solve her relationship situation. She's like, Jesus, can I get twenty minutes where I don't think about being trans, please?

Then she realizes that she's been at her table for ten minutes, nobody's acknowledged her, and actually she is literally halfway toward twenty minutes where she doesn't have to think about being trans. She makes eye contact with a waiter, he brings her a menu, she orders eggs, fries, toast and coffee. Where she grew up, this used to cost two dollars and five cents. Here it's eight ninety-five.

She takes out her notebook. She can't shut off her hetdar, though. For whatever reason she's convinced the graphic designers are going to be assholes. But when the waiter brings the coffee, she takes a sip, feels her shoulders and back tense and then relax—like, actually relax—and forgets about them. She has another sip and opens her notebook, one of those fancy Moleskine fuckers Hemingway used to write in even though Hemingway and his patriarchal, strong silent type can suck a dick.

She doesn't actually write or diagram or make a list or anything. She doodles. Since grade school, she's always been able to pay attention way better if her hands are occupied, whether it's to a teacher or a movie or her own thoughts. So she's drawing guitars, girls with super heavy dark bangs, piglets, little wax paper bags of powders, syringes, a calendar.

Syringes and a calendar because she's late for a shot of estrogen. Like, a week late.

Eureka, motherfucker. Maria is supposed to take a shot of estrogen every two weeks; some people take a pill or two every day, but she can never remember, so she shoots it into her thigh. And man, if you do not keep your estrogen levels consistent, you become a useless and fucked up mess. It's just like, it hadn't even occurred to her that she was going on romantic late-night adventures and drinking herself stupid because she needed a shot. That's good to remember. Prioritize a shot tonight, she tells herself. There was a time when she was so willful about being trans and having her shots and everything that she carried her little cardboard box with needles and bottles and alcohol pads and stuff around with her everywhere. She'd just like lay out old syringes on the table at Veselka while everybody ate pierogies, just to be confrontational. But not so much any more.

It also explains why she's been so goddam hung up on being trans. Her body is telling her, hey fucker, I am a trans body, you need to do the things that you do to take care of a trans body. Normally she's not all the way over being trans, but normally she is a lot more over it than this.

So, cool. Check. Noted.

She still has two hours to think about Steph and herself and Brooklyn and Kieran, but the bent-over little man who waits tables at six AM brings over her food and she slides her notebook aside and douses everything in ketchup.

14.

When Maria met her, Steph was this short punky femme with spiky bleachy multicolored hair and a ton of eye makeup. It was because of her more is better eye makeup philosophy that Maria developed the confidence to get as much onto her face every morning as she possibly can. But Steph was also this smart, angry little person with absolutely no sense of humor, in this way that Maria read at the time as super dykey. Maria was this trans girl whose friends were all straight dudes she'd met when she'd been telling everyone a straight dude too, which meant that, in her social circle, she was kind of an anomaly who was tolerated, not really understood or respected. She was already out, she'd already been taking hormones for a while, but when she met Steph, Maria was still in the middle of the part of transition where you get harassed by strangers.

It was at a Christmas party somebody from the bookstore was throwing, but it was an interesting one because usually bookstore parties were mostly straight people. Like, queer people from the store would come and get wasted with the straight people because in neobohemia everybody's cool with queers. But parties would usually be at straight folks' houses and all their non-bookstore straight friends would be there. It was different the night Maria met Steph: this queer girl from the art department who'd leave in March to work at Random House was having a Christmas party at her big art-dyke loft collective apartment, way out past the end of Bushwick. That meant queer people Maria didn't already know, kitschy Christmas decorations, a whole other vibe than she was used to. A vibe she'd known was out there without really knowing how to access it. As a theoretically straight theoretical guy, she had probably hung out with more dykes than the average straight guy, but it still wasn't the sort of space she felt welcome in, or felt like she had access to, or really even felt like she belonged in. Actually it was kind of terrifying, not knowing what the unspoken rules in a space like that would be, or whether any of the queers at the party would be the kind of queers who had weird stuff against trans women.

So Maria felt like she was walking on eggshells all night, wanting to make a good impression and not say the wrong things to anybody—with an unsteady grasp on what the wrong things even were—so she kind of stood by the wall with a bottle of wine, trying to look like she wasn't trying to look cool. Which is hard to pull off—she wasn't totally succeeding. Folks came and hung out by her for a minute, she'd take the occasional lap around the party, but it is hard, man—being trans, at that point in a transition, it was characterized by this intense feeling of inferiority toward pretty much everyone. Look at all these girls, they know how to dress themselves, they know how to stand, they know when to talk and when to be quiet. Maria felt like she didn't. She'd internalized this idea that trans women always take up too much space, so she was trying hard to disappear.

She had mostly quit smoking, since you're not supposed to smoke on estrogen, but in situations of excruciating awkwardness like that, all the self-invalidation and depression/anxiety, you make exceptions. She climbed up to the roof where everybody has been smoking all night. It was freezing. Like, too cold, the kind of cold where you can feel the rungs of the roof ladder through your mittens, but it felt good. Her whole face felt all rosy with wine.

She lit a cigarette and looked around. The city spread out in every direction, propping up the old moody and tragic and melodramatic mental self-portrait. Self-pity as respite from anxiety! Classy, Batman. Then Steph climbed up the ladder in this big, stupid knit hat, and it was a total first meeting from a Hugh Grant movie, like where Keira Knightley doesn't like him at first. Except in her memory Maria's not played by Hugh Grant, she's played by, like, Milla Jovovich or somebody.

Except Milla's kind of short, right? Maybe Maria is Keira Knightley and Steph is played by Milla Jovovich.

Steph didn't even want to talk to Maria. She was drunk and she didn't have a lighter but Maria didn't want to light Steph's cigarette for her because she thought that might be, like, patriarchal, somehow? Like that's what a dude does and women don't do that for each other. Who fuckin' knows, it made sense at the time Maria handed Steph the lighter so Steph had to take off her mitten and the glove she was wearing under it to light her cigarette. To this day Steph gives Maria shit about that.

No! Steph's not Milla Jovovich, she's like Ally Sheedy in The Breakfast Club, when Emilio Estevez is like, What's your drink, and she's like, Vodka, and he's like, How much, and she's like, Tons. She totally entertained herself while she smoked that cigarette by being flirty and confrontational and kind of mean.

When Maria was done smoking, she went back down to the apartment and left Steph up on the roof by herself to finish her cigarette, and then they didn't talk to each other for the rest of the night. Pretty inauspicious.

Plus, if Steph was Ally Sheedy, that made Maria the only other female character from the breakfast club: Molly Ringwald, the spoiled princess. It's a little uncomfortable for Maria how true this is.

15.

In one of Michelle Tea's books (maybe The Chelsea Whistle?) she writes this thing about how coffee is the greatest thing in the world, it makes your eyes bug out, it makes you want to write and produce and create and it's like speed except, something something, who can remember exact quotes. Maria's like, I'll get it tattooed on my forearm so I can remember it. The point is just, Michelle Tea nailed it like she nailed most other things: Maria's on her third cup of coffee now and she is making Progress.

She needs to be single. It's pretty obvious, right? When she's having boring romantic predictable teenage emotions riding her bike around the city instead of being home with Steph, the reason she likes it so much is that she's enjoying the tiniest little bit of freedom. She's not in love with her bike because of the wind in her face, which chaps her lips, or because she can totally handle the difficulty of riding across bridges and in traffic wearing a long skirt. She's in love with her bike because when she on her bike, she's not tied to anybody.

Further, she was dating somebody when she came out as trans. They broke up and then she was dating somebody else, and then they'd been broken up for a week when she started hanging out with Steph. She's never been a single woman, she's only been a woman in the context of relationships. Those relationships have been acting as cushions, as safety nets, enabling her not to have to figure out who she is, what she needs from her life. Anything.

And it's not like Steph's even stoked about this relationship any more. They still fuck, which is cool, but otherwise what do they do? They throw money they don't have at brunches so they can feel coupley; they sleep in the same bed most nights. This is literally every bullet point Maria can think of to write in her journal.

It's scary and sad and a huge relief.

Suddenly she doesn't feel all coffee exultant. She feels kind of tired and sees clearly that, like, hey stupid, you woke up at five AM, you are going to be exhausted all day. The graphic designers are gone. She doesn't want to be at Kellogg's any more. There's still an hour and a half untill she has to be at work.

There's a coffee shop near the bookstore. It's not a Starbucks, although who even would care if it was. Caring about Starbucks monopolizing coffee culture is for people who don't have more pressing problems.

Well. It is kind of depressing to try and kill an hour or two at a Starbucks. It's hard, all trying not to hear people yelling into cellphones, getting depressed whenever anybody pays six dollars for a drink.

Maria packs up, pays the bill, and rides across the bridge into Manhattan.

Once the sun is risen, the early morning sky feels more like skin crawling than day breaking and she's excited to lock up her bike and go to the little independent coffee shop near the bookstore. It's not even a little coffee shop though, it's huge and full of Internet terminals and magazine racks and, like, produce. Produce! Who knows how the thaumaturgy of commercial space rental in Manhattan works, but it seems unlikely that coffee and computer terminal rental and produce could possibly cover the rent on this cavernous coffee shop.

When you're kind of feeling like you don't know anything about anything, though, who cares. Whatever. How Zen. This is what enlightenment is like: it's boring.

She decides to drink coffee and blog. Why not blow ten dollars on an hour of Internet access that you could be at home sponging from a neighbor for free right now. Figuring out your life is more important than rent money.

She buys a small coffee and gives the girl her driver's license to get a computer. It's weird but nobody has ever once given Maria shit for the gender on her license, not in the five years or whatever that she's been presenting F but still an M in the eyes of the law. It's expensive to get your documents changed, plus you have to go to city hall and be like, I am trans, please put that on a record somewhere, which gets harder and harder with every minute that people aren't reading you as trans.

She's assigned computer #27. The screen faces some tables, but eavesdropping on what somebody's writing on the Internet is only interesting for a second, especially if there are large blocks of text that you would have to read. Nobody likes to read anything, even if it's somebody writing like Oh, oh oh, when I look at myself naked in the mirror I see tits and a dick it makes me ever so sad. Which is funny. You'd think strangers would be interested in that kind of thing.

Maria, of course, would never use the word dick to write about her body. It's way less traumatic to not use any words. Or a gender-neutral term like junk.

No big deal but Maria is kind of popular and famous on the Internet, but so is everybody, so it's not very interesting.

She's been blogging since she was a tiny little baby, like eighteen or nineteen years old, when being online was just starting to be demystified into something Rupert Murdoch could make money from. She figured out that she was trans by blogging. Awkward.

The Internet at that time was this big, exciting place where you could anonymously spill your guts about gender and discomfort and heteronormativity and how weird male privilege felt and lots of other things, except back then she didn't really have language for it so she just went like: everything sucks and I am totally sad. Just over and over and over and over, with minor variations and the occasional cuss word. It couldn't have been very compelling to read, but writing about it at length made her pay attention to patterns and stuff and introduced her to the first real-life trans people she met, even if they were on the Internet and didn't know what they looked like. She'd stay up all night, night after night, gushing her feelings all over the Internet until she figured out she was trans, transitioned, and wound up having the exact same problems as every other messed up, emotionally shut-off person in New York. She doesn't post there as much as she used to but she still has that blog. People read it. Kids who are figuring out that they're trans look up to her. It's kind of nice although since there are so few decent resources for trans women that aren't for rich trans women or boring trans women, sometimes being the big sister is exhausting.

Her computer is booted up and she is logging in when a man in a navy blue pea coat sits down at the computer next to her. He is stubbly.

Hello, he says.

Oh god dammit, she thinks.

Straight men are so weird. So weird. Like, she can already tell that he wants to be her boyfriend. He is sitting next to her and smiling like he knows something, or like he is intentionally trying to look unintimidating. Great.

Hi, she says.

You are doing what this morning, he asks with a Russian accent or something.

I'm going to read my email, she says, wishing she had the nerve to say: Go away, I don't want to talk to you. But that feels like it would draw attention to herself in a weird way for being too forward, and if she draws undue attention to herself this dude might figure out she is trans and then there would be a scene, except probably a small one because people whose first language isn't English tend to have their own self-consciousnesses to worry about and also not to want to draw complicated attention to themselves, too. Given the fact that nobody ever reads Maria as trans any more, though she thinks: what would Courtney Love do here? How does Courtney Love turn away the attention of strange men she doesn't like.

Then: no, even better, what would Steph do?

This is what Steph would do.

I'm posting an ad on Craigslist for people to date who also have chlamydia, Maria says.

You are funny, he says.

Yeah, she says, turning away from him and back to the computer. It works, he doesn't keep trying to talk to her. Good thing, too, because it's too early and she's too tired to deal with this dude who thinks chlamydia infection disclosure is flirting.

She feels bad for a second though. She's never had it, but it probably sucks to have chlamydia. What if she were some girl in the coffee shop who had chlamydia overheard that? Maria makes a mental note not to joke about chlamydia and never to turn away heteronormative advances with sexual-health-normative maneuvers. Seriously.

She reads blogs and writes in her own. She tells the Internet about her early night, her early morning, the haircuts in the diner, figuring out her life. She used to write in this thing, like, every day, but she's lucky if she can update it once a week any more. Although it's probably luckier not to stare at a computer all the time.

She writes.

Oh man. Can we talk about stereotypes and staring at the computer? Okay. I imagine that you're familiar with the stereotypes around transsexual women: that we're all sex workers, that we're all hairy, potbellied old men, that we're all deep-voiced nightlife phoenixes, that we're all drag queens, that we're all repressed, that we're all horny shemales with twelve-inch cocks. Sometimes the stereotypes are contradictory. Those ones are weird. Can we talk about what the actual stereotypes around transsexual women should be. The ones that hit a little too close to home to be funny.

1. We are not sex fiends, we are Internet fiends. This one is easy to understand. When you come out as trans, it's hard to tell your wife, or your het bros, or your dad or your, I don't know, bookstore coworkers. For whatever reason, though, it's pretty easy to tell some people from Alaska or California or, y'know, England. In this weird way, Internet message boards, livejournal, all these things feel like they're a safe way to talk about being trans—to exist without this problematic body you're stuck with, when you're offline in meatspace, like they used to say in the eighties, in William Gibson novels. Which rules.

But so there is this whole Internet community, which makes sense. It's maybe the best thing about the Internet, how you can access information you need, safely and anonymously, except that just like any other community, especially any other Internet community, it's become this closed-off thing, with stuff it's okay to talk about and stuff it's not okay to talk about, perspectives you're allowed to have and ones you're not, and its own patron saint.

Her name is Julia Serano and like most figureheads, she's very smart and sweet and right-on and almost entirely unproblematic, but her acolytes totally get obnoxious, taking her writings as doctrine.

Not to mention, if you are a total baby panda at Internet communities asking, like, How do I get hormones, Internet trans women are very nice: they will tell you. But when you ask a more complicated question, like say, how do you resolve a genderqueer identity with a female identity when it seems like acknowledging the restraints of female identity and then bursting them doesn't make you no longer female, just empowered, and therefore is genderqueer a privileged identity that's mostly available to female-assigned people with punk rock haircuts, in college, everybody gets all butt-hurt and you get in trouble.

Anyway, whatever. Stereotype: in love with the Internet.

2. There is a stereotype that trans women get all this male privilege all their lives, and then they

transition and take up too much space and are overly assertive and, y'know, stuff like that. And it's true: sometimes folks transition and are jerks; the flip side is, there are a lot of cis women who are jerks, too, and those trans women just join the general population of women who are jerks.

What's a lot more common, a million times more common, and what nobody ever seems to talk about, is this thing where trans women are given male privilege all their lives before transition, but they don't know what to do with it so it kind of stunts them socially.

Like, okay. Do you know any straight, male-assigned men who kind of get it? Like, they try to be feminist, but they acknowledge that it is a complicated, maybe impossible thing for a man to be a feminist, so they're respectful of women, and give space, stand back, whatever. And it would be totally great except that it leads to them never doing anything? Like they just stand back, and, say there are some books that need to be shelved, the windows are all dirty, there are boxes that need to go outside, and some kid threw up somewhere. You will start, say, carrying the boxes outside, and then when that's done, you start mopping up the puke, and he is just standing there, so you're like, What the fuck! Are you going to move these books or clean a window? And they're like, Oh, okay, totally, in this very enlightened way that gives you space to fucking do everything, except they need you to show them how to clean a window, because they don't want to do it wrong?

That kind of guy. I will admit: it's more complicated than that, right, I shouldn't be mean. Straight dudes have it kind of rough if they don't want to shake out their male privilege all over the place. But really? You don't know how to make a bed? You don't know how to fucking cook the onions and garlic before you throw in all the other vegetables?

Anyway, whatever. I have boys who are friends. I used to be one of those boys! This quiet dude just standing there trying to be helpful but really just pointlessly taking up space.

Anyway, that is what happens when you try not to use your male privilege, but don't have any models for alternatives. You withdraw. Here is the stereotype I am trying to get to: trans women try to shirk their male privilege before transitioning, disappear into themselves, and then can never really get back out to become assertive, present, feminist women.

And this is why everybody thinks we're weird.

Which is a loaded statement, right? Totally unfair and fucked up and that's why it's a stereotype I'm making up, but there's a grain of truth there. I don't think I've ever met a trans woman in the process of transition who was comfortable taking up, like, any goddam space at all, you know? You have to actively look at the women around you, if you're lucky enough to be close to any women, to figure out that women take up tons of space, however much they want, all the time—they just tend to do it differently than men.

Although not always, and I am definitely not going to pick apart the ways they're different. And there are men who take up space in a way that reads as female gender-normative, and there are women who take up space in ways that read as male gender-normative. Duh, whatever. All I'm trying to tell you is why it's fucked that there is a stereotype of trans women being all manly.

3. When we are rejected from the Johns Hopkins transgender program and not allowed bottom surgery, we all dig a well inside our filthy suburban houses, pierce our nipples, put cissexual women in the well for weeks at a time, and then skin them.

Actually, this one's true. We also all have eighties tattoos and poofy little dogs. The trans community officially put out a fatwa on Thomas Harris when The Silence of the Lambs came out, because we'd been able to keep that little tendency under wraps until he told everybody. Not to appropriate cultures.

4. Maybe there is another one. I don't know. We are all good at computers, we are all frustratingly shy, we're all murderers. I'll let you know if I think of any more.

She's got to be at work in a couple minutes so she checks her email one last time, gets her ID back and goes to the bookstore. She's going to be on time.

16.

She gets to work clear-headed, but she's starting to feel tired already. She's excited that she's resolved to break up with Steph. It's like her head has been plugged up for so long that she didn't even realize it was plugged up, and then she coughed really hard, or wasabi went up her nose, and suddenly she could hear. She kind of wants to call Steph right now but it's a dumb idea.

She's chaining up her bike when Kieran inevitably apparates.

I killed my father, he says in the dead-eyed monotone that means he's doing Kathy Acker.

Yes sure whatever fine sure whatever, Maria says back. She doesn't even feel like brushing him off.

What up yo, he asks.

I'm breaking up with Steph, she says, before she realizes she's saying it. Oops.

Dude, he says. He stops bouncing.

Maria's not sure what to say.

Um, she says.

Dude, we were fucking with you, he says. I didn't fuck your girlfriend.

What.

Steph was pissed at you, he says, because she says whenever she tries to talk to you... aah, fuck, he says. He starts bouncing again. Dude, you need to talk to your girlfriend, this is not my conversation to have with you. Fucking shit, breaking up with her. Call your girlfriend.

It's nine AM though. Maria's been up for a bunch of hours, she's had what, four epiphanies and two breakfasts, and she's got to go into work. She can't call Steph for at least an hour, an hour and a half. Kieran has bounced off and she's left wondering what the fuck she is doing. Is she still breaking up with Steph? She didn't decide to break up with Steph because Steph fucked Kieran. She realized she needed to be single for entirely different reasons. But that soaring feeling of release she had two hours ago, it's gone. Now it's a scraping feeling. Gross.

She punches her punch card and goes inside. Nods to the managers near the doors. Finds herself helping an old man who's looking for a book on some kind of airplane piloting, except he can barely walk or speak clearly enough to hear. He probably shouldn't be flying planes, so it's lucky that there's no way in hell this book is in the store. Mostly, he probably wants somebody to talk to, and Maria needs something to occupy her mind, so they traipse all over the store, up and down stairs, slowly because he leans on a cane, looking for this book they don't have. It is like a Beckett play or something. It would be great if this were a Hans Christian Anderson story and he was a magic fairy grandfather, tapped her in the face with his cane at the end of this adventure and then, ping, she knew what the fuck was going on with Steph, but it doesn't happen.

He comes in every two months or so. Maria kind of loves him, actually, even though nobody else in the store wants anything to do with him. He is always looking for a book that nobody's ever heard of, without an ISBN, which isn't even on the rare book sites online. Maria humors him for forty-five minutes and then he gives her some weird Italian candy or, for some reason, a crumbly old biscotti. They've been doing this for as long as she's been at the store, which is awkward, because he seems not to have noticed that she transitioned. He still calls her by a name that nobody else in the world is allowed to call her. He will stomp into the store, she will be wearing a dress and showing cleavage, and he will yell, Mister Griffiths! Who knows why it's charming instead of infuriating, but it's kind of nice.

So they walk around. It's nice to have a pattern to fall into when you just found out that your girlfriend, who is not a practical joke person, just totally faked you out about boning your half-annoying, half-amazing coworker.

After Maria's old man friend leaves, time stops and she can't think of anything to do with her hands. She texts Steph: Lunch?

Steph texts back very quickly: Totally. Burritos?

Of course.

17

Right after college, Maria tried to be an adult. She stumbled into a job at an insurance company. At the time she wasn't presenting as queer at all, she wouldn't even have known how. She painted her nails sometimes though, this otherwise normal bro, with like, shaggy hair and coral nails. People would actually ask what was wrong with her, too. Why would you do that, they'd ask, and then she'd try to imply that it was because she liked rocknroll or something.

So, when she gets to Burritoville, Steph's already there, with her spiky hair and pinstripe slacks. It's kind of a funny combination—all of a sudden she is this power lesbian. She's been dressing this way for a while now but Maria hasn't stepped back and noticed until now. She looks like a stranger, like someone from another department at that long-gone insurance company in Pennsylvania.

Maria sits down across from Steph at the table. Steph's face isn't giving anything away, but the fact that neither of them is being affectionate certainly is. They've been dating for years. They've been greeting each other with kisses for a long time.

Hey, Maria says.

Hey, Steph says back.

Nobody says anything for a minute and then Steph is like, I didn't fuck Kieran.

I heard, Maria says.

That fucker, Steph says.

Maria goes, I didn't even know that you knew him, past, like, y'know, Oh I recognize you, or whatever.

Yeah, Steph says. We met on Myspace, started hanging out. You and I don't talk, Maria, so I didn't get to tell you that we'd been hanging out.

She's points her fork at Maria but not in an unkind way.

It would be so awkward for Maria to get up and order food right now.

She can feel herself shutting off. Already. What the fuck, defense mechanisms, just once it would be cool to be able to stay present when something happens, but nope. It's like now Maria is watching Steph from a distance. From above. Astral bodies.

We've hung out a few times, Steph says. We didn't even kiss, but I was talking about you, and how hard it is to get through to you, close to you, to figure out where your feelings are, but the only way I know how to do it any more is to wait for you to write about it on your stupid blog.

Steph has always hated Maria's blog.

Then Maria is all the way gone and out of the conversation. The word blog. Maybe Maria can't deal with criticism or maybe when Steph gets attacky she gets defensive which means shut-offy. Who knows. Steph is explaining about how she and Kieran became friends online, how they exchanged a bunch of Myspace messages, she ended up coming clean about feeling stifled in their relationship, that she didn't know how to get through to Maria any more. This is all true, Maria's watching Steph say these things, but it's not like they're getting into her head; it's like being stuck in a state of perma-meta. Maria kind of wishes she could videotape what Steph is saying and take it in later, one sentence at a time, pausing it whenever she starts to dissociate.

Steph explains that Kieran thought she should do something brash, provoke a response, get Maria present and then talk about their relationship and how, once the courtship phase ended, Maria'd had her face in a book way more often than in Steph's cunt, but Maria's thinking: well, living in meta-analytical space is a coping mechanism, isn't it? When I was little, I internalized that I wasn't a girl, and couldn't be a girl. Not even like my parents beat gender normativity into me, the way the repression therapists recommend you do to trans kids nowadays. Just more, like, y'know, you learn from the television that a man in a dress is a hilarious, funny thing, and that he is still a man, even if he is wearing a dress, and nothing can change that, and nothing can change the fact that it's funny. Or you have an uncle who sees that you are wearing jelly bracelets, when you are six or seven years old, so he goes, Wow, my nephew, wearing girl jewelry, in a barely even mocking tone you internalize to mean: Not Okay. Being present in her body meant feeling things like: My gender is wrong, and My body feels weird, and My mind feels like it's being ground into the concrete by how bad I need to fix that.

She's so far gone into her own head, she only barely catches Steph asking: Are you even here now?

I am, Maria says. Kind of. There's a lot going on in my head, and I can't process this whole thing at once.

All I'm saying, Steph sighs, is that I didn't even mean to act like I fucked Kieran. He was just being an asshole on the Internet, taking up so much space and attention even in the virtual email computer thing, saying like, Tell her you fucked me! That'll wake her up! But then we were at brunch and your eyes were so far away, I was thinking how they're always so far away lately, how much I miss you—how I can barely get you to come back even when I'm fucking you—and I got mad, decided to provoke you. I'm sorry I lied, but I really don't know what to do.

Her voice catches and her eyes well up.

She asks: Is this salvageable, do you think?

I don't know, Maria answers, frantically trying to come up with something else to say. Her mind feels like the empty room in that Metallica video. Something snaps. Just be honest.

I don't know, she says again, but I'll tell you where I am with it. I rode to work that day, thinking about it. I went home thinking about it. I can't stop thinking about what we're going to do. Steph relaxes visibly, relieved that Maria is working on this. But I've been thinking about my bike. You know I love my bike. I've just been thinking, I don't think my bike is just this thing that sits outside the bookstore rusting, or inside the kitchen, rusting. That bike is, like, the only way I know to really be in touch with my life, with the world outside myself. It sounds totally hippie, but Steph, all I ever want to do is ride my bike, and there's a reason for that. I think I'm only happy when I'm alone.

Which was the wrong thing to say, or at least the wrong way to put that. Though maybe there is no good way to say I'm only happy when I'm alone. Steph's teary eyes spill over.

Maria says, I didn't mean that that way. I just mean, I'm barely here in my life, and I need to figure out what's not working.

Everybody feels that way! Steph yells. Then she drags her index fingers along the bottoms of her eyes, blows her nose, slurps from her empty soda.

Everybody does, it's not just you, she says.

I know, Maria says. I just... I've been thinking about trans stuff, like, all the time, and I don't feel like I can talk to anybody about it, because I totally fucking hate everybody else who's trans, and I don't want to deal with it. You know this story, Steph, I've told you about how I can't figure out a model for my life, my body, anything.

Maria's talking out loud about being trans in a burrito restaurant, which hasn't happened in a while. Her steam runs out and she slumps.

God, I don't know what to tell you, she says. Maybe I need to be in therapy, or go to that support group again.

Maybe therapy, Steph says. That support group never helped. And what am I supposed to do? Just wait for you to be okay? You're telling me things now but definitely not in a way that lets me in. Still.

Maria sighs. Okay. Let's talk about it tonight at home, okay?

Okay, Steph says.

Maria was supposed to be back at work fifteen minutes ago, but whatever. She can do whatever the fuck she wants, apparently, and nothing truly bad will ever happen.

Steph gets in her car—Maria can't believe Steph just finds parking and pays meters, here in Manhattan, every single day—and drives off. She doesn't hug or kiss or even look at Maria. They are in limbo.

Maria didn't actually get any food the whole time they were at Burritoville, and she's not hungry, but her blood sugar will drop through the ground and she'll get panicky, depressed and anxious if she doesn't eat anything. She gets a bagel on the way back. Sesame seeds, sun-dried tomato tofu cream cheese, lettuce, tomato, onion, salt, and pepper.

18.

All afternoon, her hands shake. Her chest feels heavy and she kind of feels like she could sob at any goddam moment. It sucks. She's like, why don't I have these responses when I'm actually, like, face-to-face with her? I mean I kind of know what is wrong with me, but seriously, what is wrong with me? It's so easy just to check out and leave your body. This is like an abuse thing, isn't it? Abuse survivors dissociate like this? As far as Maria knows she was never abused, but maybe repressing and policing yourself so hard for so long before transitioning can look like abuse, function like abuse. It sounds all dramatic but the funny thing about it is how undramatic it is when it's you doing it to yourself. It's just a thing you do. She thinks about looking into what abuse survivors can do to dissociate less so she can maybe adapt that to her own life but mostly she spends the afternoon running through the conversation she's going to have with Steph tonight.

She'll be honest regardless of whether anybody gets hurt, which is hard when you've spent your whole life like, I don't care if I get hurt, if this repression hurts me, I just can't transition and hurt my mom that way, or I can't upset my father's standing in our quiet little community that way. It is second nature, or maybe just her nature, for Maria to put other people ahead of herself. Coming out as trans was the first change she ever actually made to my own life that felt like it was leaving the map that was laid out for her at birth, and she only went against that grain because she felt like she'd die if she didn't.

She figured out that she needed to transition because she'd been going to work, coming home, drinking whiskey and reading, every day, week in and week out, until one evening she watched the sun go down behind the Statue of Liberty out her fifth-floor window in Sunset Park and realized she hadn't left the house all day. Then she was on her bed crying and fixating on the idea that this wasn't a life, she was living something that wasn't even a life, that she was putting even more work into hiding from being trans than actually transitioning would take. She cried herself out, poured another glass of straight, cheap whiskey—you don't just stop—and figured out how to get into a support group. She was like, this is New York fucking City, there has got to be so much support for trans women. If it's anywhere, it's here.

It turned out that it was only kind of here, at least in any way you can access without getting your hands all dirty with it. The Internet really is so much safer than anyplace else. There was a single meeting. It happened every Wednesday at The LGBT Center on 13th Street in Manhattan. She dragged herself to it and ended up going for nine months. The Center is a pretty fancy building in a pretty fancy neighborhood, so she was like, I will just try to sneak in unnoticed. She still smoked back then, which was nice to have—something to do with your hands and focus on while you walk over to your first transsexual support group meeting and feel like you will turn around go home and die if you can't stop thinking about the public humiliation of transitioning, scalpels slicing into the meat of your body, your parents telling you outright that they never want to see you again.

The meeting itself was also terrifying because there was no way to play it off as unimportant. It's a scene that's been played for comedy lots of times, but it's not a funny scene. It's also been played for pathos a couple times, too, but that wasn't right either. Like, once a week, for an hour and a half, maybe a dozen male-assigned people would go into a room and discuss a specific subject like self-esteem, or sexuality, or oppression, or something. Whatever. But it was weird, because there are so goddamn many kinds of male-assigned, not male-identified people there.

There was a much older woman who seemed like she must have transitioned a million years ago who eventually explained that she was a man 98% of the time. She just read as an old pro because she had a campy voice and a skinny frame. A heavy-set person from New Jersey with this aura of frustration and resignation told stories about small victories: wearing clear nail polish to work, leaving last night's mascara on the next day. Dignified, actually. In this totally unexpected way.

There were more folks from New Jersey than you'd expect, and everyone seemed to be older than her by about fifteen years at least. They'd go around the circle and talk. Mostly people would talk about how hard it was to be trans, or the trouble they were having with their families, or their jobs, and how impossible it seemed like it would be ever to transition. Eventually Maria figured out that half of the folks who were coming to this meeting were coming from a cross-dresser place instead of a transsexual place, that they weren't transitioning, they had convinced themselves not to, and that they were bringing bags of clothes and makeup, getting dressed at the Center before the meeting.

It didn't take long to feel all alienated from them. She came to the meetings in the same women's jeans and black hoodies she'd been wearing for years and would continue to wear for the next few years, well after she started taking hormones and asking people to call her Maria. She was still terrified of makeup, and even more terrified of looking like a guy wearing makeup. It was also terrifying to ask somebody at the group like, Hey, how do you do that? Which was a funny thing. It would take at least half a year of being out as trans before Maria got as good at putting on makeup as the people in the group who weren't transitioning. She sat silent at group and tried to feel a sense of community, but when everybody went to a diner around the corner together, in a pack for safety, she'd always bail even though they invited her. She worked five blocks away. Somebody could've seen her there, with them, before she came out, and then the world would've imploded.

So she stayed quiet at work. She stayed quiet at group. It got obvious that this was a pattern everywhere in her life: she sat back, kept company with herself in her head, and didn't really interact directly with anything. Well, except for the Internet, where you could just spew venom or, sometimes, whatever is the opposite of venom. Sugar? Antidote? Is anti-venom a thing? She could just unload to her computer, on a blog without her name attached to it, and then it was almost like a conversation. People would say things back, acknowledge that your experience was real. The Internet got her through way more than actual human interaction.

She is practically meditating on this stuff in the Irish history aisle when she realizes that she was supposed to clock out like fifteen minutes ago. She thinks: I don't talk to my girlfriend, but I do still talk to the Internet. The old pattern never left. Totally, unavoidably fucked up. Fucked all the way through. But she's still so deep inside her own head that she's got her helmet on, her chain around her waist, skirt hiked up and blinky light on when she realizes she's riding her bike. She actually only realizes it when she thumps into the back of a cab at a light. She's like, okay babe, chill the fuck out: you're super-internal and feeling damaged right now because you still have not given yourself that shot. You've been awake for fourteen hours after only one night of sort of good sleep. If you're not careful you're going to get run over by a truck or fall off the bridge.

It's hard though. She's going home to break up with her girlfriend of four years. She thinks about texting Piranha something wry about it but she is riding and she's resolved to pay attention.

Thank god for bike lanes. One time, Piranha decided that she was going to be a tough bike punk like Maria—well she decided to ride her bike more, she didn't actually say anything about being anything like Maria—so she rode her bike into the city from Brooklyn. Except she didn't know about the bike lane, she thought you were just supposed to ride your bike on the car lanes, where you are right on the ledge about to fall a million feet into the water—which is full of sharks—and the cars almost knock you off, over and over again, every time they pass. Furthermore, the sun wasn't up, so their headlights were disorienting, whipping by her head as they drove by. Also it was pouring rain. That's why Piranha rides the train into the city when she needs to go in. She brings a book.

Now that it's about to happen Maria's thinking about everything except this conversation with Steph. She should be thinking about contingency plans and stuff, for like what if something horrible happens. Should she bring home

Thai food? Too much.

She's going to show up at the apartment and watch what happens happen. It's frustrating but you can't just be like, okay brain, think. Because your brain is like, I am thinking! I am thinking at you, and then you're like, Jesus, brain, relax, I just mean, we need to think about this conversation. Do we just break up with her right at the beginning? Do we let her bring up the subject, talk for a while, and have it be an actual, present back and forth? The problem with that is that, obviously, if it's a conversation instead of a simple statement, like for example I am breaking up with you, then it could go anywhere. They might not end up breaking up at all.

But on the other hand, if she says it flat out right away, it's like, well fuck, what a shitty conversation will follow, where nobody will get any release or closure or anything. How do you work through anything when you skip through to the end. She's like, are you listening, brain? What should I do?

This is way too meta, her brain says. What a stupid way to try and figure out how to spare your girlfriend's feelings as much as possible while you break up with her.

She comes off the end of the bridge to a green light and decides to totally clear her brain, get in a little Zen bike meditation, like Bob Pirsig probably does in his stupid book, except she bumps into the back of another cab.

19.

Steph's waiting at the apartment, which is odd because she drives to work, and New York traffic means that riding a bike is usually way faster than driving. But she's on the couch, in her work clothes, with a bottle of organic red wine because she knows that estradiol and non-organic red wine don't mix. The fact that she's got the whole bottle of wine on the table, her own glass half full and Maria's empty, waiting, says that they are going to have a long conversation. A bottle-long talk.

Hi, she says, and she stands up. Hugs Maria.

I left work early, she says. Do you want wine?

Thanks.

She pours a glass. Maria wonders about food: she barely ate lunch and probably ought to eat something. Steph's on the couch now though, ready to launch in, so eating gets deprioritized. Maria's like, maybe I should have that shot first? It wouldn't really make her feel more lucid untill tomorrow, though, so a shot gets deprioritized too. She sits on the couch a thigh's width away from Steph.

Look, Steph says, I am breaking up with you.

20

Ten minutes later, Maria's on her bike again. There will be no closure, no conversation, no figuring out what the fuck is going on tonight. She slugged down that glass of wine without any food and now she's on her bike, flying down Jamaica Avenue. Piranha doesn't live anywhere nearby and who knows what her neighborhood is even called, it's just way the fuck down, south and west, toward where the signs are all in Russian and the avenues have letters for names. Maria hasn't called her yet, and she also hasn't decided whether she's going to stop into a bar for another drink or two. Probably not. The desire to self-obliterate isn't as intense as the fear of dealing with people. And Piranha is maybe the greatest fucking genius who ever lived at not dealing with people.

So Maria rides for a while, fast, until her legs hurt and her lungs won't breathe right any more, but she doesn't really know which way south or west are. She thought she'd been pointing in the right direction, but maybe she's never ridden from her own apartment to Piranha's, maybe she's always gone there from work or taken the train. Weird.

She's in some kind of clean-looking neighborhood full of two-story apartment buildings and parking lots. She's like, I bet I'm either near the ocean or in Queens.

She finds a subway station, carries her bike down the stairs and checks a map, chest heaving, face damp in the humid night. She's in Queens, near the ocean. She pretty much went in exactly the wrong direction, which is more due to the way she rides her bike than her emotional state. She tends to just point in a direction and trust that she'll get there; it almost always works. Who knows how she got so turned around, but whatever. Riding feels good so she doesn't get on a train. She lugs her bike back up to the street and starts to ride.

As soon as she's going pretty fast, she gets doored. Shit luck. She kind of bounces off, falls on the ground, bounces up, and glares at the person. She doesn't say a word to boring-looking white guy in the car, just makes a feral face, gets back on her bike, and bails. Almost immediately she's going fast again, cutting through a busy-looking intersection as the light turns yellow.

Soon she recognizes her own neighborhood, then she recognizes the neighborhood next to it, and then the next one. It's dark out at this point, and the air is all misty around the streetlights. It's like a picture inside a New Jersey punk record from the nineties, all serene and lonesome and pretty. Her face is kind of wet and she starts to worry that it's going to rain for real, that she's going to show up at Piranha's with a total butt stripe. It doesn't though. It's just misty.

Turns out Piranha's neighborhood is really far away, though. Inevitably Maria runs out of adrenaline. She stops at a red light, even though when there's no cars you're supposed to totally blow through stoplights to show how anarchist you are. She sort of starts to process the conversation she and Steph had half an hour ago. Ambush! While Maria was freaking out about how to have that conversation Steph figured out how to communicate more directly than either of them has ever done before.

There wasn't much to say after that. Maria was like, I was going to break up with you, too, and then they just kind of looked at each other. Steph cried, and for a minute Maria felt like she might not, and she felt heartless and mean down to the bottom of her lungs, but then she cried too. Just a little. They hugged and Maria said something about figuring out logistics tomorrow but that she had to go get drunk right now. Steph laughed, which made Maria feel like probably one day they'd be friends.

Dykes.

It feels shitty not to have gotten to say all the shit that Maria is just realizing she needed to say about patterns of checking out in her own life and stuff, but *I am not your girlfriend any more* is pretty close to *I don't have to listen to your shit any more*, and plus, who actually wants to say those things out loud? No matter how bad you need to.

The light changes and Maria realizes, Wait, shit, hold on, I am elated. It's that feeling like you just left on a car trip for Arizona or Michigan or something, and you don't have to worry about rent or work or feeding the cat or anything at all for a whole week. Except there's no time limit. I don't have to take care of myself. Or sleep. Or bathe! This might be kind of a bad news train of thought.

Past that stoplight the road goes downhill for a really long time and her bike feels like a Pegasus or something. It's trite to say you feel like you're flying, but it's like flying. She spreads her arms out like Kate Winslet on the bow of the Titanic.

At the bottom of the hill is the edge of Park Slope. Piranha's house is still like miles away and even though it's not raining the mist is soaking through her clothes so Maria decides to take the train. This is the actual reason that she doesn't know the way on her bike. It's a pointlessly far ride. She realizes she's gotten bored right around here before. She's a catharsis biker, not a distance biker.

Plus, on the train, you get to read books and drink whiskey, so she stops in a liquor store and buys a flask. She doesn't want to be drunk, but she does want to be drinking. It occurs to her to text Piranha.

Um, Steph broke up with me. Coming over.

She gets on the train without waiting for a reply, because what's she going to say, no? Plus, Piranha's not going to be doing anything, she hates everybody way too much to go out when she doesn't have to.

The Q train is pretty full because it's a Tuesday night and people who work in the city live in fancy two-story homes out by Piranha, so they're all on their way back. Maria gets into the role of dirty punk with bright fake-colored hair, taking up too much space, smelling bad and drinking whiskey. Like, she's known real crusties, and she is not a real crusty, but in comparison to these investment bankers, she's like, Boxcar Bertha.

She's also excited to be reading a book called *Big Black Penis*, which is about masculinity and black men. She holds it up high so everybody can read the title. It's for the best that she rarely feels excitement like this, because she's kind of being confrontational about it.

The train rolls on, the people empty out, and then she's at the Avenue Z stop, so she tucks the book in her bag and hauls her bike out. Piranha's texted back, Shit, okay. Do you want beer?

Piranha rules.

21

Apparently Piranha was going to that trans women's support group for some of the same time that Maria was, but Maria doesn't remember her being there. Piranha remembers Maria, she says, because Maria looked as terrified and mousy as Piranha felt. Piranha transitioned way before Maria did. The way they met was, the year Maria decided to go to Camp Trans, Piranha responded to the same Craigslist rideshare post Maria did and they ended up carpooling in somebody else's car. Maria thought Piranha was a total bitch at first, but that's fine, Piranha thought the same thing about Maria. Neither of them ever lets anyone else in. It's like they have matching armor. Or complementary armor. Piranha kept making mean jokes the whole time, and Maria kept sleeping. Neither of them had driver's licenses. Maria is such a tough crusty bike punk that she let hers totally fucking lapse. Anarchy.

Eventually they bonded over some band or something and then they were friends. Maria's the only person who calls her Piranha. Everybody else calls her Melissa. People kept confusing the two of them that week at camp, so one night Maria got drunk and decided that a nickname would help people differentiate them and that Piranha was a good nickname for a former hardcore kid turned sweet but angry lady who was still kind of a hardcore kid.

She uses the word agoraphobic for herself, but it's not clear how literally she means it. She works at a Rite-Aid in her neighborhood out here, instead of at a fancy bookstore in the city like every other pretentious fuck. She doesn't like to be far from home. Her story is long and complicated, but the takeaway is that there's this trope that trans women are these fragile creatures who are getting killed all the time. Who are easy to kill. But if Piranha's an example, trans women are actually some of the hardest motherfuckers in the world to kill. She's one of those good people you hear about to whom bad things happen. Her health tends not to be so great. She takes a lot of medication. She's generous with it.

Once she explained that it's usually way cheaper to get painkillers, or antibiotics, or anti-depressants, or, like, hormones, anything at all, from somebody on Craigslist than it is to get them from shitty drugstore employee insurance. Plus, nobody on Craigslist wants to thoroughly psychoanalyze you to let you continue taking the hormones you've been taking for seven years.

It's the sort of thing a badass older sister would tell you. At some point Maria and Piranha's friendship settled into this kind of big sister / little sister dynamic, where Piranha's the smart experienced restrained one and Maria's the younger more outgoing one who's always flipping out.

Maria rides from the train station over to Piranha's apartment, which is a small bedroom with an even smaller kitchen attached and the smallest bathroom in Brooklyn. Your legs actually stick out the door when you pee, and then you use the kitchen sink to wash your hands. It's underneath the stinky kitchen of somebody's nosy Polish grandparents, but Piranha's one of the only broke people in New York who can afford to live alone and the apartment is actually really nice. She takes care of it: there are plants, tapestries, an acoustic guitar, and an ancient computer that can still play DVDs. When Maria visits they mostly watch movies.

Piranha opens the door after one knock. She's wearing a long Indian-looking skirt and a baggy brown jacket, both of which hide her figure. She gives Piranha a hug and she says, I'm so sorry, babe.

Maria says, Yeah, thanks, it's cool.

Piranha goes to put a beer in Maria's hand but it clinks into the whiskey bottle that's already there. Piranha laughs.

Maria goes inside, closes the door, and Piranha says, Okay, go.

What do you mean, Maria asks. The air in Piranha's apartment always feels kind of thick, like they're baking pierogies or something upstairs all day long, and tonight in the weird autumn humidity it's a serious relief for Maria to strip off her jacket, her hoodie, her scarf, and then her long skirt.

Maria Griffiths, Piranha says, one time you came over to my house and immediately processed for half an hour about a new coat you'd just gotten. It would blow my mind out of my head if you weren't just bursting with revelations you wanted to tell me about.

It's funny that you'd just start in like that, Maria says, because that's kind of the reverse of what I've been thinking about. I am a vocal person. I talk too much, right?

Yeah, Piranha says, on the Internet.

Whatever, Maria says. But I hadn't been talking to Steph, like, at all. For like two years I couldn't think of anything to say to her, but I had shut myself off so badly that I didn't even notice.

Yeah, Piranha says.

I mean, for fuck's sake, I cannot shut off my interior monologue without booze or pills, which sounds totally rocknroll and so high school at the same time, doesn't it?

It does, Piranha says. She pauses for a second and then goes, Rocknroll and high school are kind of the same thing, though.

Totally, Maria says, feeling the tension seeping out of her back. She flops over onto Piranha's bed. Thanks for letting me come over.

Well, you didn't really ask, she says.

Maria's like, Haha, fuck.

So go on, Piranha says.

Okay, Maria says. Here is the thing: I have a million bajillion trans things that I need to figure out, still. I am totally the Buddhist monk who's all convinced she's attained enlightenment! The day you're convinced you've got it is when the older monk needs to pop you in the head and tell you that you are a stupid baby. And the fact that I haven't been able to talk about my shit at all is that pop in the head.

Piranha smirks but she doesn't say anything. It's cool that she just lets Maria perform.

I'm just at this point where I'm stomping around like I know everything about everything, just because I transitioned and now creepy old men on the street hit on me—when really, I'm stunted back at like age thirteen, age five, age zero, when I first started suppressing stuff I knew I couldn't say in public. Like, y'know, that feeling without words that I had my whole life like oh my god something is seriously fucked up with my body and the way everybody is reading it.

Yeah, Piranha says.

I'm just like, I need to be single for a while! So badly! I haven't been single and transitioned at the same time ever in my whole life, and how am I supposed to have unfucked-up relationships with people if I've never done that? So I am excited about that. On my bike on the way over today I felt like I was flying. My lungs are all full, I feel like I can breathe—all the end of the Lifetime movie things.

So you're getting totally wasted to celebrate.

No, I'm getting totally wasted because she broke up with me first! I figured this all out, decided to break up with her, scheduled a time, and then she was just like, I am breaking up with you. What the fuck.

Oh yeah, Piranha smirks, you decided all that on your own, and you picked the time to meet? You asserted yourself like that?

Whatever. Kind of. I don't know. Do you want a shot?

No, she says, I can't really drink hard alcohol any more. But go for it. Do you want a shot glass?

The ritual appeals and Maria says yes. Then she thinks: ritual, shot, fuck! I am getting later for my injection with every passing moment, which explains the mood swings.

Oh shit, she says, Piranha, I am late for my shot.

How late, she asks.

Um, like, a week and a half?

Oh fuck, she says, laughing out loud and handing Maria the shot glass.

So expect mood swings tonight, Maria says. She fills the glass and then drinks it.

Fuckin duh, Piranha says.

An hour later, Piranha's probably said a dozen words, and Maria has said a thousand times that. Piranha's nodding and listening, asking open questions to get Maria to go on, but eventually she's just repeating herself.

So basically, Piranha says, your development is totally stunted, and what you need is the kind of adolescent adventures you didn't have when you were younger.

I guess so, yeah.

Okay. So. You are single now. Do you want to have lots of sex with lots of people?

God no, Maria says. Are you kidding? How am I going to do that, and how am I going to do that with my junk the way it is, and anyway: bio-cock.

Piranha spends a lot of her time reading the Internet, so she's super up on, like, everything. She probably doesn't go to sex parties, although Maria hasn't asked. But she's talked a lot about this thing where there are lesbian sex parties that happen in the city and how they will often have No Bio-Cock Policies, meaning, No Trans Women. Or, optimistically, Trans Women: Keep Your Pants On. Meanwhile trans guys are welcome to brandish whatever cocks they want. Kind of frustrating, kind of problematic, and deeply representative of Maria's own issues with her junk—even if she's never actually had a partner who had issues around it. The term bio-cock has become shorthand for the fact that trans women aren't sexually welcome in any communities anywhere.

Yeah, Piranha says. Bio-cock.

They've been on her bed pretty much without moving for an hour or so. Maria stands up. Stretching her muscles feels good, and she's suddenly grateful that she didn't just immediately get totally trashed.

What were you up to tonight, Piranha?

Heroin, she says.

Really?

Yeah.

Do you want to tell me about that?

Obviously this is significant, but it's not really a mind-blower. Piranha's always got pills. She's always got something going on, some kind of illegal Robin Hood self-care. But obviously it's kind of a big deal. Heroin's the cul-de-sac at the end of Drug Street.

Maria, Piranha says, you are not the only one with problems.

The subtext is like, hey Maria, the world is an asshole to me all the time and you haven't even asked how I am.

Fuck, darlin, she says, I'm sorry. What's going on?

Piranha flops heavily down onto the bed and sighs. You know I've been saving for bottom surgery for like a decade, right?

Yeah.

And you know I've got a fuckin chronic pain fucked-up health thing or whatever.

Yeah.

Well it never occurred to me until this week to look into whether one would complicate the other, she says. And it turns out they do. Pretty bad. The surgeon I wanted to see won't even touch somebody whose body breaks down like this. My second choice won't either. The only one I can find who will do it is really fucking expensive, in Thailand, and not particularly reputable.

Shit, Piranha, I'm sorry.

Yeah, she says. So it's like, I kind of doubt I'm ever going to have a vagina. Which sucks. So I'm indulging.

I didn't know you had connections for—Jesus—Heroin.

Craigslist, she shrugs.

So what do you do, shoot it?

Nah, she says. A needle in my leg every other week is too many needles for me. I snort it.

Yeah, Maria says. She sits back down on Piranha's bed, but gently. One of the first things they bonded over, in the car on the way to Michigan, was serious fear of injections and how weird it is that the desire to get estrogen into your body can trump that fear. But every time, both of them stare at that leg for hours, listening to album after album, before they can actually stick that needle in and inject.

Injecting heroin, of course, makes Maria think of high school. Doesn't it make everybody think of high school? In the Cow Town she had a friend who hated everything. Like, he was a racist, he was a misogynist, he hated queers, he hated his parents, he hated school, he hated movies and music and hippies and jocks. Obviously mostly he just hated himself. He worked in the receiving department of a Wal-Mart, carrying heavy stuff around, and every couple weeks he took all the money he made at that job into Philadelphia, spent it all on heroin, brought it home, and shot up two or three times a day until he ran out.

Pretty classy.

But they were friends. Eventually Maria figured out in therapy that their friendship worked because she was emotionally shut off trying not to be trans and he was emotionally shut off being an addict, so they could hang out and be emotionally shut off together. He was always trying to get her to shoot up, too. She never did it though. She snorted lines from his bags a few times and once or twice she gave him twenty dollars to bring back a couple bags for her. She never got hooked though. She'd do it once or twice and then wait a week, terrified of losing control, but a little bit fascinated by the glamour of it. It was the era of heroin chic.

So Maria is aware that heroin totally rules. Like, being asleep rules, and being high on heroin is like being asleep times twenty. You just feel at rest. Mostly she would snort five or six dollars worth of heroin and lie face down on a carpet somewhere, hoping not to be disturbed, eventually puking somewhere.

She stopped doing it when she left town for college, stopped talking to people where she was from and stopped having a connection.

Piranha is explaining the justifications that surgeons

have for not operating on people with endocrinal and immunological situations like hers. Maria's just looking at her face, though. She's gorgeous, but not the kind of gorgeous where you want to shove your hand down her pants and your tongue into her mouth—the kind of gorgeous that you want to marry and keep next to you all the time. Her cheeks make up the majority of her face; her eyes and hair are the same shade of brunette, two shades darker than her skin; her lips are full enough to match her cheeks. Some trans women mostly date other trans women, but Maria probably isn't strong enough to handle shared trauma like that. But for a second she wishes she could date Pirahna.

Fuck, darlin, she says again. I wish there was something I could do.

Yeah. I wish people would come if I had a benefit. Like trans guys who have top surgery benefits? Fuckers.

Haha, she says to Piranha, yeah, it's pretty much you and me against the entire world.

You and me against the rest of the queer community, she says back, only she's not really kidding.

23.

They watch movies. Heroin isn't cocaine; Piranha doesn't do more than one or two more lines all night, and she doesn't chatter away. She actually looks way less stressed than usual, just kind of lying back, watching zombies eat faces and monsters destroy New York, but not really responding to anything. Maria falls asleep. Piranha probably does too.

Then the sun is coming up through her one small semi-opaque window. Maria snaps awake and realizes that she has to go to work. She carries razors and makeup with her; she runs the water until it's hot, gets a presentable shave, does her eyes, and checks in on Piranha. She's sleeping calmly, chest rising and falling, same clothes as last night. It's awesome that she's got this moment of peace; Piranha really does have way more shit to deal with than she deserves.

Maria, on the other hand, leads a super-charmed life. Steph broke up with her, she went to her friend's house and got drunk, and then this morning she doesn't have anything worse than the same headache she has every morning. Jesus. She considers riding her bike all the way to work, but that'll take forever from out here, so she buys a coffee and a bagel and gets on the train. She kind of resents spending two dollars on a Metrocard, though.

Mostly what she's taken from her conversation with Piranha last night is that she needs to be extremely irresponsible in her life from now on.

She has a journal! An honest-to-god paper notebook journal like our ancestors used to use. Fully aware that she is going to get coffee all over herself, she arranges her bike, messenger bag, coffee, and bagel in a way that lets her write in it. She ends up scalded and stuff, but whatever, she hasn't written in this thing literally in a couple years except for the doodling she did at Kellogg's the other night. Maria reads so much that she assumes one day she'll have an idea and put together a Great Anti-American Novel or two, so she always carries it. Mostly it is phone numbers and addresses and doodling, though.

OCTOBER 15TH.
Piranha's on heroin.

She can't think of anything else to write, though, and after four and a half words her hand is starting to cramp. She can type all night, but with a pen, not so much. Maybe she should keep a haiku journal, in a non-appropriative way. It wouldn't be appropriative to write like Hemingway.

OCTOBER 15TH, PART 2.
I am a soldier in the First World War. I don't have
very many feelings. I drink a lot and girls like me.
We had a long conversation about whether she
should have an abortion, but we didn't use the word
abortion. The whole thing was a dream and
I am dead.

It's the sort of dumb, self-conscious stuff she used to write when she was a kid and nothing really mattered. She used to get stoned and write about vampire dinosaurs, or write a review of a rock show for the school paper without mentioning the band's name at all except in the headline. She's been single for twelve hours and she's already regressing back to sixteen.

She wonders what she's going to do after work today. It feels exciting.

24.

She almost kills everybody getting her bike and stuff off the train in the morning rush but whatever. You can't help but look cool carrying a bike up subway stairs, and then she's on the street and it's pouring. It had been gorgeous out by Piranha's house. She doesn't have an umbrella, but she does have a hoodie, so she pulls up her hood and says fuck it. Rain rules. She's all ebullient, and weirdly can't wait for her lunch break so she can write in her journal again.

There is always construction everywhere in Manhattan, which means that it's easy to find a spot under a tarp overhang thing to chain up her bike so it doesn't get rained on any more than it has to. She goes into work, regretting a little how wet she is, but whatever. She clocks in, finds a radiator way back in the Irish history section, and throws her hoodie over it: fire hazard schmire hazard. The Irish history section rules because almost all of the books' spines are green and because it's around two corners from everything else, which means the managers never really go there. Like, if they do, they will catch you trudging your way through John O'Driscol's history of Ireland and scowling, but they almost never do. Mostly it's just the occasional lost customer. Or Irish person.

When the air is humid from rain like this, the humidity mixes with the dust that's literally all over everything in this store and you can barely breathe. It means you need to take a lot of breaks, leave the store a lot, you know? Maria goes on her first walk at 9:45. She's like, maybe pizza for breakfast?

This is Manhattan and tons of pizza spots are already open. Breakfast pizza is irresponsible to her belly, and she can't afford to get a bagel for breakfast and then also pizza plus coffee and then, later, lunch, but also, whatever.

Irresponsibility. Maria's never been irresponsible. When she was little, she was responsible for protecting everybody else from her own shit around her gender—responsible for making sure her parents didn't have to have a weird kid. Of course, then they had a weird, sad kid anyway, right? Whatever. That's when responsibility at the expense of self became a habit: she did not care about school, but she knew her parents would be sad if she didn't go to college, since certain things are expected from you when you do well on standardized tests, so she scraped by and paid attention. Then, with drugs, it's like, she took them all, but always in such moderation that it wasn't really dangerous. Even when she was throwing up or incoherent, it was in a controlled situation. She never went to jail, never had the police bring her home, never got caught breaking curfew or went to the hospital or anything. And then she came to New York, paid her rent, had a job, kept her head down, had relationships with people where making the relationship run smoothly was more important than being present in it. Which did not work. It's clear that being responsible has not been a positive force in her life. It has been fucking everything up.

She buys a vegetable slice and walks back to work in the rain. Further, being irresponsible totally works out for her. The only way she's been able to keep this job and not lose her shit completely is by taking lots of trips outside, spending lots of time reading instead of working, helping wingnut old man customers for hours at a time even though they're not going to buy anything. Or riding her bike dangerously: she got doored yesterday, her hip is still sore, and guess what, that is a pretty good story. Or even this morning, on the train! She spilled coffee all over herself, took up tons of space, and ended up reminding herself how much she enjoys writing total bullshit in her journal.

She's like Sigmund Freud: she can come up with a million examples to support whatever bullshit theory she wants to support. And being completely irresponsible for the first time in her life is so appealing that she is fully willing to build a case for it.

She's the Sigmund Freud of Irish history.

When you are trans, you are supposed to know everything about men and everything about women and the ways they interact and the important differences that lubricate the dating book market and how ultimately everybody is fundamentally the same but also fundamentally different. And when you first transition? For the first couple years, you totally think you do. You have dated girls all your life, but as a boy, so you have this experience of knowing what it's like to be a straight boy, but now you are a girl, and, more and more, the world is seeing you as a girl, and also the girls you are dating are now relating to you differently than the other girls you used to date used to relate to you. Also, now you've been on a couple dates with boys, so you feel like you are this great authority on what it's like to be a het girl. And you just want to talk about it, all the time, because it feels like such a revelation: oh, now I get to act this way on a date, and oh, now I have so much insight into why my old relationships would always fail, I am Nietzsche's fuckin' uberlady, and oh man I am so smart all the time I just want to tell everyone how the world is.

Then, after you have felt very smart and insightful for a long time, you start to realize that all your insights are kind of stupid. For one thing, when you were supposed to be a boy, you weren't, really. You learned how to act that part, the way your culture taught you (and it was pretty easy), but your heart wasn't really in it. There was an undertone of mopiness to your performance and experience of boy which isn't really there for most boys who aren't trans. Then, you figure out that when you first started spending more time with women in a non-sexual way, they weren't treating you like a boy, and they were letting you in kind of similarly to how they normally let other women in, but you were this effusive, messy, uncertain person of indeterminate gender who was prone to freaking out and having breakdowns over things like, say, boys giving flowers to your friends but not to you.

And then, when you dated that boy those two disastrous times, he knew that you were trans, and you will never know whether that informed the way he treated you, which means that for sure you were a lot closer to a heteronormative girl-boy relationship than you'd ever been in, but how are you going to relate that to anybody else's experience?

Then you started dating dykes and found out how different it was to be a girl who dates girls than it was to be a boy who dates girls, but you could never really separate out whether it was because the girls you were dating now were different from the girls you had dated previously, or whether it was because dykes were somehow fundamentally different to date from straight girls, and then further: really? You dated one boy so you're going to talk about what it's like to date all boys? On top of which, you dated what, three, maybe four girls before you transitioned? And they were all pretty different from each other, had different issues, different ways of dealing with relationship stress, and now you're going to generalize about all women?

On top of which, sex has always been super problematic for you. Even before you knew you were trans, it stressed you the fuck out. You thought you were into it, you definitely liked the orgasms. It's not like you had any reason you knew about to be mad at your junk, but jacking off was always way easier and less stressful than actually getting and maintaining an erection when somebody else was there. And further, you didn't even know you were dissociating during sex until you'd been doing it for about a decade. You'd heard about dissociation a lot of times, and then you finally put together that, actually, that's what it was when you had to stop paying attention to the person you were fucking so that you could fantasize about any number of situations that didn't have anything to do with having a penis and fucking somebody with it. So you have no idea what it's like to have a loving relationship with fun sex in it, which you assume everybody else has. Although really how are you gonna know?

And those are just the relationship aspects of gender. What about the way you get treated by old men working in stores? Young women? Do you think being tall, thin, and white has anything to do with the way you're treated now? Do you think being thin, dressing okay, and being white had anything to do with it before you transitioned? There are so many variables that it's like, you see all the constructions, all the connections, and you kind of understand them, but if you ever plan on trying to make sense of them, you'd better be doing it in a cave on a mountain someplace far away from other people, where you can eat lichens and drink from a shallow mountain spring and meditate eight hours a day—because it is very complicated.

But still, Maria is like, I'm supposed to have some kind of insight? Here is my insight: gender is stupid and annoying and I don't want to talk about it any more ever. And if somebody is super-stoked to use me as an example of how gender isn't real, or if anybody ever wants to talk to me about how my body is an example of genderqueerness at its most integrally crucial, or if anybody wants to tell me that they are through with their first year at a women's college and that they represent the End of Gender, then that person can fuck off. Kate Bornstein was right when she said none of this gender stuff is real, but she didn't go far enough. All of this gender stuff is stupid and it's so complicated that it's impossible to make sense of.

A tall, fiftyish gentleman type wanders into the Irish history section, all but bumps into her, then takes off his hat and bows subtly but dramatically. His clothes are clearly expensive.

Pardon me, my lady, he says in this Upper East Side drawl or something.

Of course, Maria says.

He looks at the shelves for a second, then seems to catch himself. He turns to her and he says, Forgive me for saying so, but you are beautiful.

Aww, thank you, she says, suddenly playing the sweet het girl.

Have you read all of these books?

He is being playful. Ugh. She mumbles a no and turns away, still smiling because what else are you going to do, explain patriarchy to this fucking rando?

He turns to look at the books again, and she start to walk around the corner, just so she doesn't have to awkwardly interact with this middle-aged suitor, but he stops her with his voice.

I'm sorry, but may I ask you a question?

Of course, she says.

Would you join me for lunch this afternoon?

No thanks, she says. I have a boyfriend.

Then she pretty much runs away.

Obviously she should have told him she was gay. And that he was too old for her. She should have said a bunch of things, but one, she has frustratingly internalized the social code that says younger women must not be rude to older men, and two, disclosing that she's gay always feels like it's necessarily going to lead to the person figuring out that she's trans, and not only does that feel scary and kind of dangerous, but it feels like they also might want to ask whether she's really gay, if someone who is Really A Man and dates women isn't just some fuckin creepy dude. Part of transitioning is trial-and-erroring your way through the social interactions that most women trial-and-error their ways through around puberty, learning just how to make a rando who's hitting on you go away without getting mad. But when you're twenty-nine and you haven't learned this stuff, it feels impossibly mortifying.

So it's actually way easier just to humor these men who grew up watching movies where the girl doesn't like the hero until he's been persistent enough to make her like him. This is the grease that keeps the gears of the heteronormativity machine spinning, obviously, but it's just easier to slip out of an awkward situation with an awkward guy than it is to call out the misogyny inherent in what he's doing. It's a tough spot to be in, but also, this is coming from an angry dyke who's also trans and who, at one point, had society try to use her as a vessel for that kind of misogyny. So.

It's irresponsible just to propagate that, but also, what tools do you have to dismantle it? Male privilege sucks and is weird and the fact that it exists, that you've even had the experience of people trying to give it to you and, to some degree, have internalized it, complicates the decision to be totally irresponsible. Like, if you're irresponsible, doesn't that just give people like Johnny Upper East Side something to take advantage of? Or do you just do irresponsible within boundaries, so fuckers don't end up figuring out you're trans? That doesn't feel like irresponsibility any more, it feels like contained rebellion, which is as productive as bringing a skateboard into the mall or wearing Chucks to church. A t-shirt with a cuss word on it.

On the other side of the store from the Irish history section Maria starts doing mental calculations about how to fit the word Irresponsible across her knuckles. IRSP NSBL? Maybe. That looks kind of stupid though.

Now that she feels weird and afraid to go hide in the secret Irish history cave, Maria decides to leave the store again. She's walking, who knows, somewhere, and it's pouring, so she's trying mostly to walk under awnings. She still gets soaked, but whatever.

It's not really problematic if your irresponsibility doesn't affect anybody else. As long as this newfound freedom expresses itself as doing stuff that doesn't hurt anybody else, doesn't make anybody else feel awkward or oppress them, it's probably fine. There are Adderalls in her purse. Under the awning of the Halloween store she takes two.

NOFU TURE would fit across her knuckles. That's kind of the right idea, but the Sex Pistols? Also totally unproductive teenage rebellion, the t-shirt with the cuss word on it again. The problem is, how do you have some kind of emotional catharsis when you know you're too old for it? The trick, of course, is rejecting the poisonous, normative idea that there is a Too Old For Catharsis. Or, really, a Too Old For Anything. But rejecting normative ideas about age is as hard as rejecting normative ideas about gender.

Now she's six blocks away from the store and since she's just going for a walk to clear her head, she turns, walks another block, and then heads back.

She is soaked when she gets back in and Thomas McNealy, the manager, is waiting for her. He is a dick. He's got to be in his mid-fifties, he's got a wife and a kid, and he's been working at this store forever. He is the gruff grownup, the one who tells you that you're fired or that you're on probation or whatever. He seems to like his job, too, like he's been stuck here while the bohemian dreams of his youth burned down to a nine-to-five at a shitty bookstore and he wants to take it out on somebody.

Where have you been? he asks.

I went to get a bagel, she says dumbly.

Where is it?

I ate it.

You ate the whole bagel, he says. Did you get permission from a manager to go?

She thinks about lying and then admits that she didn't.

Maria, he says, making sure to draw out her name in a way that makes it clear he remembers it wasn't always her name, You have been late almost every day for months, and now you are just leaving without permission. Please clock out.

25.

And that's that. You could be melodramatic and say: just like that Maria Griffiths is homeless and unemployed in New York City. The reality though is that she has a bunch of places to crash, so it would be appropriative to call herself homeless.

Okay, she says, great! I'm just gonna grab my stuff from the back, and I'll be on my way!

All cheerful.

Someone will bring you your things, McNealy says.

Haha, you're really not going to let me go back to the closet to get my bag?

You don't work here any more, he says, looking off to one side, already bored with this conversation.

Some new kid brings her bag up. They must have watched her leave and prepared for this. Awkward, but whatever. Once again her response surprises her: she's kind of excited. She laughs in the old fucker's face, takes her bag, and walk back into the rain. She practically knocks over the terrifying owner of the store who's just arrived in a cab or a car service or whatever. Right on time for work at noon.

Oh, she says, looking all disdainfully at Maria. This woman hates all of her employees. That sounds like a petulant thing to say, but really, you'd be hard-pressed to find someone at the store who can remember her ever saying anything nice to any of them. She sure doesn't seem to care about books. Who knows why she continues to be involved with this store, unless it is like a next-level capitalist appropriation of and capitalization on the work done by the oppressed, in the same way that the kids in Brooklyn are appropriating its history, in the same way that the kids with Macbooks in coffee shops on the Lower East Side are soaking up and erasing Keith Haring and the Ramones. And this woman always seems miserable. When Maria was presenting as a boy, she was indifferent-to-mean; then, when she started presenting more queerly, she became a target. She would single Maria out whenever they were in eyesight of each other. Don't you have something else you could be doing? she'd ask, or Will you please rearrange these books that don't need it for no reason except that I want to tell you what to do? It was almost like a Mary Gaitskill kind of sadism, except that Maria didn't see her often enough for there to be much of a narrative. Also, she's never used the right pronouns. Maria has actually gone up to her office to talk to her about it, but it has always ended in an awkward stalemate. Which feels better than letting it go—but the fact is, she is too rich and important to have to acknowledge anyone who works for her in any way.

Maria yells, Yeah! Oh!

Shouldn't you be inside working? the owner drawls at Maria, totally bewildered.

I just got fired, Maria says. It occurs to her that she could continue, tell her what a horrible person she is and that all of her employees loathe her—this is the exact moment every union member wishes for, the chance to cuss this woman out—but really: like she doesn't know that everyone resents her. Maria looks into her dead eyes a second longer than would be comfortable, then shoulders past.

The older woman doesn't say anything, she just goes inside.

Maria starts immediately to regret that she didn't get a jab in, but whatever. She's outside in the rain and she's got the whole afternoon to herself. The whole week, actually.

It hits her again that she's pretty excited not to have a job any more, even though that means no more money until she can find another one, and no more health insurance. Who cares. She never has to go back to that job she was so indifferent about for so long because she absolutely, completely hates her life in New York.

Whoa. Sometimes your internal monologue surprises you.

She thinks about going back to the apartment she is probably still sharing with Steph, but seeing all Steph's things would be kind of rough right now. Then she thinks about going to hang out with Piranha, but she is probably going to be asking Piranha if she can crash at her house a lot pretty soon, so she'd better not just start taking up space there immediately. She could go see a movie, but suddenly being broke is a lot more real than it was a couple hours ago, and ten dollars for a two-hour distraction seems pretty irresponsible.

Like, bad irresponsible.

She decides to go to Alt.Coffee. It is this biggish coffee shop on Avenue A where they have computers and stuff, but also couches and expensive coffee and atmosphere. It's cooler than the coffee shop by the bookstore. Like, in a gentrification sense.

As a last act of epic brutal punk rock defiance, she steps two feet back into the door of the bookstore and grabs an umbrella out of the umbrella basket. Ha! She leaves her bike chained up outside the bookstore, under the awning where it'll stay dry, and walks the six long blocks to Avenue A.

It's so grey out. It rules. This has been her favorite kind of weather since she was a little kid; she loves going inside after being in the rain, when you're kind of wet and cold but you immediately start warming up, and you finally start to feel just how wet you are as soon as you start to dry out. And then you can look outside and see the rain, watch it run down the windows, and nobody can realistically ask you to go outside and play.

New Yorkers walk by and ignore her; cabs splash puddle water everywhere; nobody waits for the Don't Walk sign to turn to Walk before they cross the street; rain looks like it's freezing to the frail branches of the city trees. Maybe the rain will start to freeze, turn the sidewalks icy. It's fall, so it might happen, but it's very early fall, so it might not.

This umbrella is enormous and it's got a Nike logo on it. Punk rock indeed, Batman, she says to herself as she retracts the umbrella and goes into the hip coffee shop. They have an umbrella bucket and she worries for a second about whether somebody will steal her umbrella, then laughs at herself. Who cares. It would probably do her some good for somebody to steal her stolen umbrella so she would have to walk back to her bike in the rain. She thinks about how good a hot shower feels when you're soaked in cold rain.

UMBR ELLA, she thinks.

She didn't bring a book and she doesn't really know what she's going to do at the coffee shop. Spend money on Internet access to look at help wanted ads on Craigslist? Her résumé from years ago is probably somewhere in her email. She could update it to include this most recent job, act like she left without being fired, lie and say a friend is a manager who thinks she was a great employee. She can use her real name, not her legal one, and just not freak out about it if anybody asks—just tell them she's trans at the interview. If she gets an interview. That way it'll be out in the open, at least with the management, at her new job. Which will be as somebody's assistant at a publishing company or something. Who knows.

She gets a three-dollar drip coffee and gives the barista her license. She doesn't look at it, but she's got dyke hair so she probably wouldn't care if she saw the M. Maria is assigned computer number 23, but after fifteen minutes of looking at Craigslist her eyes glaze over and she's falling asleep sitting up. She doesn't have the energy to email that girl. She does not feel like job searching. She's like, do I even want to stay in New York?

She doesn't actually have to.

She goes back up to the counter, tells the girl that she's done on the computer, and gets her license back. Five dollars for fifteen minutes. She takes her coffee over to a couch, sits down, and takes out her notebook.

OCTOBER 15, PART 3.
I hate New York, but I love the New York rain in autumn. Like, the November rain? But it is October and I just got fired from the stupid bookstore. I didn't even cuss out whatsermonster. Now I have to figure out what the fuck to do with myself. Do I get a new job in Brooklyn, near my apartment? Except I am going to have to find another apartment, too.

I am exhausted from thinking about being trans all the time and I wish I could stop. If you work for the City of San Francisco, dear diary, did you know that they will pay for bottom surgery for you? It might be an urban legend. Maybe I will look into it.

It didn't even occur to me to go out and get drunk after I got fired, which is interesting. It's almost like I got drunk all the time when I was dating Steph and working a shitty job not because I am a total addict, but because it was a coping mechanism to deal with being unhappy.

Her hand hurts already. It sucks that being from the computer generation means she can't write longhand, like, at all.

She texts Piranha, Can I stay with you again tonight? Got fired a little.

She puts the phone back in her pocket, but it rings immediately. It's Piranha. She stands up to go outside because who cares what everybody else does, who cares that there are only three other people in the coffee shop at two PM on a Wednesday, it is rude to talk on your phone when other people are trying to concentrate.

Dude, Piranha says.

Hi, Maria says, maybe more cheerful than she actually is.

I'm working tonight, but you can come get the key from me at work and stay at my house while I'm out, and like, take a shower or whatever.

Thanks, Maria says.

But listen, you can't just stay at my house all the time, you know?

Yeah. I was—

Piranha cuts her off. I know you know, but it's like, dude, Maria, besides the occasional text, I hear from you once every two or three months, because you're so occupied with your girlfriend all the time, and now suddenly you want to hang out all day every day because you don't have to worry about her any more? That feels kind of fucked to me.

Shit, yeah, I—

No, listen, Piranha says. I'm not gonna put you out on the street, especially if you just got fired from work. And I want you to tell me all about that. I'm not super-pissed at you or anything, I just need you to understand that I feel kind of resentful about the fact that you've ignored me pretty bad for so long and now that you've got a reason besides that you're excited to hang out with me, suddenly we're besties or whatever.

Okay, Maria says, probably hurt the most deeply that she's been in these last couple days.

I miss you, Piranha says, and I am excited to see you again, but I needed to put that out there. I've gotta go to work at nine, come see me then, okay?

Yeah, Maria says, okay. They hang up.

Now her mood has come back to earth and she feels like shit. Maybe she should get a beer.

Turns out they have two-for-one beers after four at Hi Fi half a block away, but Maria doesn't wait until four. Then, when four o'clock hits, she has her third and fourth beers, then falls asleep on the bar for a couple hours. Who knows why the skinny, pretty bartender lets her sleep. That's kind of off limits at most bars. Maybe having a transsexual pass out at your bar for a couple hours is just the kind of gritty authenticity that a bar on the Lower East Side needs now that everybody's moved to Brooklyn.

26.

Maria wakes up and has an idea. It's a drunk and stupid idea, but she doesn't really give herself time to think about it. Steph broke up with Maria, so Steph probably feels some kind of good will toward her right now. She will probably let Maria borrow her car. By the time she gets to Brooklyn she'll be sober enough to drive, and the thing is, Maria doesn't want to be a drag on Piranha. She'll ask to borrow Steph's car for the evening and then take it for a trip out of town for a few days. Kind of an asshole move, but whatever, New York's public transportation system is the best in the world, it would do Steph good to take advantage of it for a few days.

Who cares where she goes. Upstate New York? A rest stop on the Jersey Turnpike? The sky is the limit. Maybe characterizing her new lifestyle as irresponsible isn't right, exactly, but instead she should be justifying acting on every dumb idea she has as a very enlightened, Buddhist kind of living in the moment.

She kind of doesn't want to have a conversation with Steph, though, checking in about feelings or whatever, so she texts: Can I borrow your car tonight?

Maria wakes up a little more. There are maybe a dozen people in the bar now, way more than there were when she got here.

Steph texts back: Sure, spare key's in the kitchen. How you doing?

Maria gets into it as shallowly as she can: Okay. Letting out some shit. Y'know.

Steph doesn't text back.

That umbrella is still at Alt.Coffee—she was already half asleep while she stumbled over to Hi Fi. Nobody stole it! She unfurls it and walks the seventeen fucking avenues or whatever it is back to her bike, then takes her bike down into the subway and rides back out to Bushwick. She's resentful again that the rain is making her pay two dollars to ride the subway: the main reason she started riding a bike is that the subway is expensive.

On the L train, she finds a seat, sits down with her bike next to her, and feels it in her back, in her shoulders, in her neck, and even those weird, thin little muscles in the back of her head that are obtusely connected to her jaw or something. She's been postponing exhaustion because of the good bad things that have been happening, but really she just wants to have some place to rest, just to pass out for a few hours. Her apartment is not that place; Steph is probably there right now, although maybe not. If she goes to Piranha's house, she might not be able to decompress before they are talking about what an inconsiderate friend she's been—even though Maria knows Piranha well enough to know that she's said her piece and now she's done with it, and they don't have to talk about it more unless Maria wants to. But Piranha's working tonight. At nine, which means she won't be back to her place untill the sun comes up tomorrow morning. If Maria gets the car, rounds up her estrogen and the bike rack and maybe some clothes for a little trip out of town, she can totally go crash at Piranha's place for a bunch of hours. I have options, she's thinking as she passes out on the train.

By virtue of never really sleeping deeply, always being tired, and having lived in New York for a long time, Maria has the New Yorker's sixth sense about subway stops. She wakes up as the train is slowing down for her stop, actually feeling kind of rested.

Outside it's not really raining any more. Or, more precisely, it is only kind of drizzling. It's mostly mist, like the fog that was around the streetlights last night. It's gorgeous. I'm going to miss you, Brooklyn, she thinks, letting herself realize that she's actually, like, leaving leaving.

Letting herself realize is an interesting way to put it— she's kind of deluding herself, again, already. Automatically. If I'm ever going to be not fucked up, she thinks, I need to be honest and explicit with myself. So: I'm going to go upstairs and lie to Steph, tell her that I want to borrow her car for the evening, when really I am going to take her car for a few days, maybe a week. Then, I'm going to drive down to Piranha's work and get her house key from her, so I can sleep at her house for a few hours. Also, probing around in what she's hiding from herself, she realizes: I'm going to get the contact information for the person she got her heroin from. I like heroin, and I miss it, and I'm not going to shoot it, so I am going to get a bunch and bring it with me when I leave town, hole up in a hotel for a while and obliterate myself. I don't want to die or anything, but I need a clean break from my life for the last four years, six years, twenty-nine years. For sure.

Plus, what could be more irresponsible than a wee heroin bender rebirth ritual.

She chains her bike to the railing of the steps at the door of the little apartment building. She doesn't need to carry the bike up the narrow stairs because she's going to take it with her on the back of the car. Last night was actually probably the last time she'd ever carry her bike up those stairs.

Steph isn't home. Maria looks around the apartment, again kind of melodramatically, like this is the last time. Since Steph's not here, she actually could take a minute to round up some stuff and bring it with her, but what is she going to take—her computer? The cat? She stuffs some underwear, a second bra, extra razors and shaving cream, her shot stuff (fuck), into a giant duffel bag, grabs the car key off the counter, and leaves. She doesn't need to bring food or anything, because, okay.

Further honesty? Her bottom surgery fund is not enough for bottom surgery. Like, tens of thousands of dollars of not enough. And she's going to be living on that money until she gets another job, which means, eventually, starting over with saving up. So she might as well enjoy blowing it. On heroin. And on gas, maybe even to get off the east coast. On maybe driving as far away from New York City as she can get.

The Bouncing Souls do a song called 'Lean On Sheena,' about a girl leaving her abusive boyfriend and how nobody's ever going to see her again because she is leaving. Maria feels like Sheena. Her whole life is the abusive boyfriend she's finally leaving, and everybody is rooting for her.

27

Steph is at the bar down the street, a charmless little hole in the wall that's either so hip or so unhip that it's just kind of boring inside. The bar runs the whole narrow length of its single room. There's obvious rock music in the jukebox, boring beer posters, and art by shitty local artists on the walls. She's drinking top shelf scotch because it's hard to break up with your girlfriend, even when you know the relationship is over. And this is the first time in her life that she can afford it, even if she does have half a bottle of wine at home.

She's taken one of Maria's weird old paperbacks from one of the shelves that line their apartment because she realized, right after Maria texted, that sooner or later she wasn't going to have access to all of Maria's books any more. She's been trying to get into it but she can't focus. It's a story about a girl in New York who's a knight, and she's friends with a dog, or something. It's weird. She feels like you could just flip to a page and start reading. There's no plot.

It might be a good idea to text Kieran and ask him to meet her here, but actually, that is obviously a really stupid idea. She doesn't know who else she could call, though. She and Maria have built up kind of an airtight life together, and you can't just call up the friends you ditched to be in a relationship and expect them to run straight to the bar. Or can you? Maybe that's what friends do. They give you shit about not having called them in two years, then buy you a shot and then hold you while you cry and cuss all night. She's probably never had friends like that. Now she has coworkers who are okay though. Maybe she could call Karen or Sonya or somebody, but that seems like a bad foot to start a friendship on. Or maybe it would be a good foot? Who even knows any more, who can tell? You lose perspective when you disappear into a relationship. She's got to remember this shit in the future.

The main thing that's for sure is that Maria borrowing the car for a night is going to turn into borrowing the car for like, a week, where she's going to have some weird and epic adventure that doesn't really make sense to anyone who isn't her. By the end of it Maria will feel like she's really accomplished something and like everything is different now, like she's figured out her shit. Only nothing will change. Some version of this has happened every autumn for the last three years and Maria, of course, has no idea that it's a pattern.

This time they're broken up, though, and that's not changing. It's obvious that neither of them is growing any more in this relationship; in fact, that's been obvious for a long time, which is why Steph's actually decided to start to have a career, a life—a wardrobe that she likes, instead of a wardrobe as a weapon. Maria couldn't hang. She talks a lot about punk rock this and punk rock that but Maria's never been in a band, never collected vinyl, never been to a political protest, never even had a stupid haircut. Her quote unquote punk rock ethics are vague and privileged holdovers from the straight white boy outsider stance she took for the first chunk of her life, and they've never been challenged or put to any kind of test.

Same with her sexuality. While it's been obvious for years that she's been faking her orgasms, it has not been obvious how to get her to stop, to give in and be vulnerable and present for sex in the moment. Part of that, of course, is that when you're a cis woman you can't just demand that your trans woman partner get comfortable with her own body, her own frustrating anatomy. But another part is that after a while when your partner is faking her orgasms, you stop caring. You think for a minute, maybe I should start faking my orgasms too, but that is depressing if only because it would mean only ever actually getting off by yourself. But it turns out that using your partner basically as a sex toy to get yourself off—suspending disbelief and convincing yourself that she's hot for you, that she's into it—is even lonelier than never getting off.

So what do you do?

Who knows what Maria is hot for, what kind of kinks she has. Maria herself probably doesn't know. No matter how clear Steph has been about the fact that no kink could possibly be too shameful to admit, even something horrifying you'd never actually want to do in real life, Maria won't fess up to anything. It's hard because Steph has understood for a long time that your kinks aren't arbitrary things your brain comes up with. They're not coincidences from childhood that you fetishize. Or: they could be. But kinks are arrows giving you directions. If you're hot for being whipped, that probably says something about your relationship to guilt and punishment, or pain, or something. If you want someone to slap you and call you a stupid little girl, that probably says something about your relationship to ever having been a little girl and feeling stupid for or about it. It's always complicated and emotionally volatile but there's also no reason to be ashamed of it. Maria says she's a pervert and stuff, but Steph hasn't been able to get specifics out of her since they first got together. Even then, those specifics were, like, bottom, and bondage, and vague single-word clues like that. Maybe she's into guys. Maybe she can only get off by literally being killed. Who knows. Steph's been checked out of this for so long that she's definitely not going to figure it out tonight.

This is her shit, of course. Latching onto a relationship and trying to make it work. It was like this with Rae, with Leah, with LL. This is the fourth relationship in a row where she's looked up and realized that she's been lying and faking for three months, nine months, two and a half years. Next time, she swears, no fucking around. No caretaking. No self-sacrificing. Next time she's going to date somebody whose shit is all the way together, who can communicate clearly where she's at and what she needs.

Steph thinks: I need to read *The Ethical Slut* again and then not date anyone for five years.

Like, obviously transitioning is hard and being trans is hard, in ways Steph will never be able to understand. Maybe being trans just means Maria can't get off. But the self-protectiveness around sex extends to literally every other area of her life. She won't check the balance of her checking account unless the ATM refuses to give her money; she fixates on the possibility of having bedbugs for months before she'll even lift the mattress and look for eggs. She's been working at the same job she hates for more than half a decade because she's afraid to look for another one.

Sometimes it seems like being trans is the only bad thing that has ever really happened to Maria. Like she's got a turtle shell to keep anything bad from ever happening to her, and with that shell there she can't move. Probably what Maria needs more than anything is for something pretty bad but not catastrophic to happen to her. Maybe this breakup can be that thing, but probably not. It sounds like Maria's already spinning it into an opportunity for self-mythologizing instead of for learning or growth or whatever. Which Maria will go on to talk about when she meets her own next girlfriend. *Here is what I've figured out about myself, here is how emotionally honest I can be, here is how vulnerable I am.* With cussing. Maria will be funny and kind and hot and all the things that make you fall in love with her and maybe her new girlfriend will call her on it, the moment she starts to shrink into herself and disappear, the moment she starts phoning it in. Her next girlfriend will be clear, Either get present or get the fuck out.

Maria, of course, will get the fuck out.

Whatever though, it's easy and obvious to sit and wish something bad would happen to the girl you just broke up with. A more productive question would probably be like, Well Steph, what do you do now? You have no prospects, no desire to get into a relationship immediately, no goals, and an apartment that's suddenly twice as expensive as it was yesterday, because there is no question that Maria's going to want to move out, if only because she certainly can't afford this apartment herself. There are five months left on the lease, and for the first time ever Steph actually probably could afford to live in an apartment in Brooklyn by herself.

She sees the words By Herself in neon behind her eyes when she blinks and then she can't get rid of them. She's not going to cry though. She orders another Laphroaig.

Outside the window at the front of the bar it's hard to tell if it's mist or rain and she's certain her dumb girlfriend— her dumb ex-girlfriend—is getting soaked and feeling lonely and romantic about it.

28.

The drizzle has turned into proper rain again as Maria is strapping her bike to the rack on the car's trunk. She gets soaked. Her denim jacket was already soaked, and she doesn't really have a heavier jacket. You don't need a heavy jacket when you layer: tank top, collared shirt, hoodie, jacket, scarf. Of course, they're all soaked. She gets the bike attached and locked and tries to figure out whether she should put plastic bags or a tarp or a blanket or something over it, but fuck it. Whatever. She's a tough bike, she can get a little wet.

Steph's car is a little green Civic from about a dozen years ago. Relatively fancy. Clean. There's a CD player, a radio, a blanket, a water jug. They used to go on road trips sometimes. It's been a while.

She clicks her seatbelt, lets out the clutch and realizes, Fuck man, how do I get to Piranha's neighborhood again?

One time Steph observed that Maria tends not to be very performy, and when she is performy, it's almost always for herself, not for anyone else. She thinks about that as she's pretending to push buttons on an imaginary GPS on the car's dashboard. It's a problem, you grow up reading about punk and grunge and earnest dude rock in all the magazines and internalizing the idea that artifice is totally bullshit, man, and we wear these clothes because they're comfortable, not for any kind of fashion statement, and we're just trying to communicate, not be cool, and then you transition and realize, oh shit, there is going to have to be some intentionality in the way I present my body and my actions. I am going to have to break the patterns of clothing and voice and hair I've had in place all my life if I'm ever going to be read the way I want to be read. Like, it would be nice to believe that you could just exist, just be some true, honest, essential self. But you only really get to have a true honest essential self if you're white, male, het, and able-bodied. Otherwise your body has all these connotations and you don't get the benefit of the doubt.

It's like the Buddhist thing where the Zen master goes, Show me your true face, and the student goes, Sure, here it is! And the Zen master goes, No, show me your true face, and the student goes, No, seriously, I am, this is my true face, and then the Zen master goes, Get the fuck out of my house, you are not showing me your true face, and then the student goes AAAH I AM SHOWING YOU MY TRUE FACE WHAT TRUE FACE ARE YOU EVEN TALKING ABOUT NOBODY HAS A TRUE FACE and takes a swing at the Zen master and the Zen master dodges it all easily and sits back and goes, ahh, there it was, you don't have to leave my house after all.

There's probably more to it than that, but what Maria took from that story when she read it was: frustrated angry face is true face.

So she's driving to her friend's work, to crash at her house with, like, semi-permission, in a semi-stolen car, and also she's planning to buy a bunch of heroin and split town.

That feels good, it makes her laugh out loud. She has two CDs in the car. One of them is by Fugazi. She turns it up. She's sixteen, but she's the right sex this time, and it feels mostly liberating and exciting but also a little sad. You can't help but feel sad for fucked up, confused, couldn't figure out which way was up inside her head little sixteen-year-old Maria. Not just sadness, but like this enormous empathy; I feel for you, kid, but I swear to god, your life is going to get better than you can imagine right now.

Forty seconds after getting all excited she's tearing up a little. While she starts to cry, Ian MacKaye yells his head off and guitars scratch at the speakers. Maria is in love with her life and her bad intentions and kind of excited to be gone and mostly excited to get a shot into her body. She is not going to forget to give herself that shot when she's at Piranha's, she'll make herself remember so her feelings can get back to normal, her tits can stop aching, her head can clear up.

She finds her way to Piranha's neighborhood eventually. She stays close to the BQE without actually getting on it because that thing will fuck you up. She'd also just rather drive around neighborhoods, waiting at lights, looking at stuff and listening to music, than sprint over there all fast. Whatever. First it's Bushwick, then she's in Williamsburg kinda, then Bed-Stuy, then on the other side of Bed-Stuy it's like Park Slope, where the rich lesbians and white people with babies dressed in forty-dollar sweaters live, and then it's... who knows, maybe this is Cobble Hill? Some other neighborhood, and then some other neighborhood. The buildings are getting shorter and further apart and then she's in Piranha's neighborhood.

The area reminds her of Cow Town, Pennsylvania, in a surreal way. Like, obviously, it's not mostly woods and farms and sparse highways, but there's an impressive diner where old people eat breakfast 24 hours a day, and there are people dressed in impeccable clothes from the Gap or Aeropostale or, like, the Nike store and other kinds of places that are only in malls, and cars that look kind of new but not very new, fluorescent-lit dollar and thrift stores. Whatever. It just feels way less urban than the rest of the city. Which is fine, just weird. There's also a beach in Brooklyn. Brooklyn is this huge and variegated city of its own that became a part of New York City in the Great Mistake of 1898. Maria learned all kinds of stuff about Brooklyn when she got here because when she moved here it wasn't Cow Town and she fell in love immediately.

Piranha's job is that she is a cashier in a drugstore. She likes it because she doesn't have to be responsible for much, she makes enough for rent and food, and she doesn't have to leave the neighborhood. Once she told Maria that if her job didn't make her interact with people she didn't know, she would never really talk to anyone. It's a free-standing building with its own parking lot on a long, wide street of low buildings and parking lots.

Maria parallel parks the car on the street right out front and goes inside. Her heart races for a second because of how many times she came into drugstores when she first transitioned to try and secretly buy makeup, without anyone knowing, convinced that everyone was staring at the trans person, knowing she was trans, judging her, and cracking their knuckles before they beat her up. Nobody looks at her though. Piranha's the only one behind the counter and there's a long line, so Maria goes to poke around for a while.

There are these Precious Moments figurines, they're like porcelain, little kids with giant eyes handing each other a heart that says LOVE on it, or rolling around with a puppy? Maria stumbles into a whole aisle of them. Tears start welling up in her eyes, again, which is totally not tough and totally not punk but which also you totally can't lie about. Like, they're depictions of this idealized childhood innocence, right? This idea that little kids have the potential for sadness in their giant eyes, but really they just know these pure emotions: love, happiness, whatever. It's totally hokey and stupid and obviously a construction. Real little kids are as dirty, impure, and complicated as the adults they're going to grow up and be. But this sort of thing gets her all melodramatic and choked up specifically because of how fucked up she was convinced she was when she was little. She didn't know she was trans, she couldn't put into words that she was a little girl, but she did know that something was horribly wrong and she blamed herself for it. Other kids could stomp around and punch each other and sleep at night, but she was this self-conscious mess who liked books a lot because sometimes people in books seemed as bewildered by the world and themselves as she was. She was never a little kid who could get a puppy and be happy about it. If you'd given her a puppy, she would immediately have started worrying about what if she trained it wrong, what if it ran away. She would already be sad that it would die.

She looks at the porcelain things for a second. Kids' moms had kept these in glass cases in their living rooms where she grew up, so they're also kind of a sad reminder of the Christian culture that raised her, which she's rejected. She stops herself. She wipes tears away, one on each side, and goes to see if the line to Piranha's checkout is still there. It is. She is ringing somebody up but she sees Maria's puffy eyes and goes, You're not allowed in the Special Moments aisle, Maria. Then she throws her keys at her. Who knows why Piranha has so many keys on there: the garage opener, the fuzzy thing, the prickly rubber thing. It's more of a bog knot of stuff than a key ring.

Do you have a break any time soon? Maria asks.

Nah, she says, Not for a few hours. You okay?

Yeah. I think I'm gonna get out of town for a couple days.

You gotta get one of those iPhones, Piranha says, scanning a box of tissues. Keep your Internet constituency updated.

Fuck my Internet constituency, Maria says, The whole problem is like, feeling like I owe my Internet constituency some fuckin—

Piranha rolls her eyes hard at the woman she's ringing up. Right: she's at work.

Sorry, Maria says. But listen. I was just wondering. You remember the Craigslist thing we were talking about last night?

Piranha's eyes widen for an instant, then go back to normal.

Forty-nine forty, she says to the woman she's ringing up, and then to Maria, Yeah, how come?

I was just wondering if I could get that number, she says.

It's an email, she says. She swipes the customer's credit card and then scribbles an email address on a scrap of register paper. It ends in 420.

Okay, thanks, Maria says. I'll see you in the morning?

Sure thing, she says, already ringing up the next person. Maria had forgotten that they were kind of in a fight.

29

Back at Piranha's house she emails the guy. Writing an email asking for drugs is complicated because you don't want to talk about how, y'know, you're trying to buy a bunch of drugs, but you also don't want to use a bunch of doofy, vague language: Hello, I would like some of the Stuff my friend got from you, can I come over please? After parking outside Piranha's place, throwing her bag and coat on the floor in the kitchen and deliberating for a while, though, that's pretty much the email Maria sends. She worries that dude's not going to get back to her tonight, which would kind of wreck her plans to be gone forever in the morning, but he emails back right away.

How do I know you're not a cop, he writes.

She emails back: I don't know. I'm not a cop. I'm a girl who's grumpy and leaving New York forever and wants to bring a bunch of. Um. Stuff with her.

How much, he emails back. They are basically instant messaging via email, like our ancestors did, but maybe you kind of expect weird behavior from drug dealers. It's been a while. Maybe this is what it's like now.

I don't know, she sends. Like four hundred dollars?

Come over tomorrow morning. We'll still be up.

He sends his address, which is in Williamsburg. He's probably some rich white college kid who comes from money and thinks he's untouchable. Maria hadn't thought to ask Piranha what he was like.

Rad, she emails back. She sets her phone alarm to wake her up a little before Piranha gets home, only realizing much later that avoiding Piranha is consistent with the social and emotional rampage she's been on, and lies back, excited that it's not even ten yet and she's going to get some actual sleep. She puts on a movie about a monster who lives in a river, and every once in a while he flips out and, like, physically rampages, killing or kidnapping people. It's a pretty good monster. She doesn't make it to the end, but it's fine, she's seen this movie before.

30

She wakes up with the alarm in the morning with a single huge thought in her head: I didn't get my shot last night. She considers getting out of the apartment, maybe doing her estrogen shot in the heroin dealer's bathroom, maybe getting it in the car at a rest stop in New Jersey. Then she decides that, no, this isn't the exciting irresponsibility she was thinking about yesterday. Not giving yourself your shot is like slamming your fingers in a car door over and over, or forcing yourself to drown a kitten every morning or something. Totally unproductive.

She keeps her shot stuff in the cardboard box they mail it to her in. If you've got a prescription, you can actually get it pretty cheap; rule out the surgeries she can't afford and being trans is more or less affordable. It probably works out to about fifty dollars a month, just for the testosterone blockers she takes twice a day and the estrogen she injects every other week. Theoretically.

She puts on shaving water to boil and sits on Piranha's bed. She cleans off the bottle with an alcohol pad, pulls the estrogen into the syringe with an 18-gauge needle, flicks out bubbles, switches out the 18-gauge needle with a 23-gauge one. Then she cleans a spot on her thigh with another alcohol pad, cleans it again, picks up the needle, and breathes heavily for a minute.

It's very, very hard to inject yourself with a needle. She hates it and will never get used to it. This moment right here is the reason she's so fucking late for her shot. The excitement that comes with the beginning of transition has worn off and now this is just a shitty thing she has to do to herself sometimes. She pictures Piranha walking in after work, after giving Maria the email address for her heroin dealer, and seeing Maria giving herself an injection on her bed. She would know it was estrogen, if for no other reason than that Maria is injecting it into a muscle instead of a vein, but she would still say something sardonic and mean and hilarious. Then she pushes the needle an inch deep into her thigh, pulls the plunger back, and injects. It doesn't really even hurt.

The water boils. She shaves, puts on makeup, and digs out a pair of jeans from her bag, not because she doesn't feel like wearing a skirt any more but just because she feels tougher in jeans and she's going to be traveling soon.

The drug deal in Williamsburg is totally uneventful. Dude is right off fucking Bedford Avenue, in this huge, fancy converted loft building where rent probably costs fifteen hundred more dollars a month now than it did fifteen years ago. He has sideburns and a tastefully ripped t-shirt, counts out forty bags, takes the four hundred dollars, and that's that. They even say thank you.

Her hip creaks when she gets back into the car and she realizes she hasn't even looked at the cool bruise she's probably got from when she got doored.

She tucks the drugs into a sock, tucks that sock into another sock, tucks them into the bottom of her bag, and stuffs that bag into the trunk of her car. Then she texts Steph: Please don't kill me, but can I borrow your car for a couple days? I will owe you forever.

Steph texts back: Whatever.

She's had her shot and she's got her drugs. She drives into Manhattan over the bridge she's ridden her bike over every morning for the last six years. She turns up the volume on the same Fugazi album she's been listening to since she was sixteen and makes her way to the Holland Tunnel. The sign says Holland Tunnel: STAY IN LANE.

Fuck this, she thinks. Fuck this city. Fuck this coast. What if I just go to fuckin California or something.

PART TWO

LATE NOVEMBER

1

Star City, Nevada is fucking bullshit. James grew up in the worst fucking town and he still lives here and he's probably going to die here. It's stupid. It was a boomtown in the late 1800s, all beefy cowboys and ladies of the night or whatever and then everybody realized there was no fucking gold here and left for California. Then nothing happened here for a hundred years, it was just a shitty little stream dribbling down between two shitty little mountains until sometime around when he was born, in the mid-nineties, when the Wal-Mart corporation saw an opportunity for brand infiltration and blew a hole in the side of one of the mountains and put a little bridge across the middle of the parking lot so the stream could run through the middle and differentiate the Star City Wal-Mart from every other Wal-Mart in the country that doesn't have a stupid fucking stream running through it.

He actually kind of likes the stream.

As soon as there was a Wal-Mart in Star City, the people who got jobs at the Wal-Mart needed places to live, so they built these shitty condos down the length of the stream and then when all the waterfront property was taken up they started paving streets away from the stream until they practically almost had a fucking town here. Almost a town, definitely not a city.

There's a truckstop out toward route 80 and a couple stores that aren't Wal-Mart (a shitty little florist, a shitty kind of big garage), but mostly since Wal-Mart sells everything every other shitty little store would sell anyway, this town is like: there is a mountain with a Wal-Mart on it. Then there are a bunch of stupid buildings on the hill spread out beneath it. Then there are some more houses around where the ground flattens out. There's a steep road that goes straight down the hill and a less steep road that swerves around the long way down the hill and last year they put in a GameStop and a Subway and six empty stores in a strip mall between the highway and the Wal-Mart. But mostly what they have is dirt and dust and nothing and majestic boring vistas and bored asshole teenagers and stars. The name of the shitty little town makes it sound like celebrities would vacation here or something, like in a dumb cop show from the seventies or a two-dimensional stage set from an old black and white movie, but really the only reason to name this shitty town Star City is that at night there are so many fucking stars above it.

As long as you're facing away from the Wal-Mart.

2

That's the big picture. That's Star City from above, the establishing shot, how it looks from the outside—not that James would know. The furthest outside Star City he's ever been is Reno, like, four times. If you're from Reno, Star City probably looks like some debris and nothing next to a mountain. But if you grew up here, it's probably because your parents moved here to work at the new Wal-Mart when it opened because there were no fucking jobs anywhere in Nevada in the mid-nineties. Or something? Unless you wanted to deal blackjack in Reno. But neither of James's parents wanted to work in a casino. Whatever. Who cares. James grew up here and it is stupid, fuck Star City.

The small picture, the tight shot, the closeup, is that James is stoned as hell, reclined in the flimsy plastic tub with the black grout or whatever the fuck it is called, the moldy stuff that seals the tub to the floor and the wall. He is hotboxing the bathroom of his apartment halfway down the hill from the Wal-Mart. Right now he is too stoned to tell if the water is hot or cold: it is probably lukewarm. Who knows. He sits up and looks at the mirror and can't see anything because there's so much smoke in here and also because that shit is all fogged up from how hot the bathwater was, some impossible-to-know amount of time ago. He's thinking about how much he hates Star City and why it produces such apathetic and useless fucks: figure 1: James, figure 2: Nicole. But mostly he's just stoned and spacing out.

He keeps coming back to how cheap this bathroom feels. This town sprung up out of nowhere and they built these shitty apartments out of bullshit but it's weird how even though he feels numb about pretty much everything else in his life he can't quite get accustomed to his shitty apartment. The material of the tub against his bony ass feels like you could get up and punch through it. Brittle plastic, brittle bones.

James smokes weed specifically so he can think about his ass against his bathtub and not about the fact that his girlfriend Nicole left an hour ago, stormed out in an angry huff. He's in the bathtub because on some level he knew that if he hadn't given himself a project, immediately, he would have followed her out of the apartment, out into the parking lot, and made amends. Apologized, patched things up. But she's right to be mad: there is something wrong with him. He has no idea what the fuck it is, but he does need to figure it out if he's ever going to have a normal human relationship. So he was like, Well, I'll hotbox my bathroom and think about it. He's working on it. He gave himself a job.

He left his phone on the bed, went into the bathroom, and blocked the crack at the bottom of the door with a towel, an old habit from getting high at his mom's house when he was fourteen that he didn't even realize he didn't need to do any more. He made sure he hadn't at some point accidentally put the batteries back into the smoke detector, ran a bath, and blazed the shit out of ten or twenty dollars worth of weed. He even used the bong, not one of the pipes. Smoked the buds, no shake. The plan was to smoke until there was no air left in the bathroom. To smoke until he could see through time. To smoke until he figured his shit out.

And he is figuring his shit out. Everybody knows that smoking weed is hardly the path to self-knowledge or anything. It's probably the path away from self-knowledge, unless self-knowledge is, like, thinking about establishing shots in Stanley Kubrick movies. It is not. But this shit is seriously better for figuring out his shit than sitting on the couch with Nicole, again, watching some dumb movie she wants to watch because all the movies James likes are 'creepy' or 'gross' or 'impenetrable' or whatever.

He should've brought his iPod speakers in here or something. Even with smoke instead of air in here it feels shitty to think about this stuff. Fuck feelings.

3.

Eventually you have to come out of the bathroom. Eventually the water goes cold again and he's already topped it off with hot water twice. Hot water is included in the rent so there's no reason not to just keep doing this until he falls asleep or dies, but also James is legitimately bored and stewing and he imagines getting out of the tub, stoked to open the door, hurry out of the bathroom, and watch all the smoke billow out of the bathroom like the van in *Fast Times At Ridgemont High* or a Cheech and Chong movie. He sits in the tub while it drains though. Now he's legitimately cold. He gets up, wraps a worn-out towel around himself, throws the door open, and rushes out.

The smoke pouring out of the bathroom is a disappointment. There's smoke, and it sort of rolls out of the bathroom, but it's not that thick and it doesn't really seem to be in a hurry. It's like when you're smoking and you imagine you're in a rap video and all this thick smoke is seeping out of your mouth all slow, but then you see yourself in the mirror and you just have a stupid expression on your face and look like an idiot who can't even fucking smoke right. That kind of smoke. That kind of feeling. Suddenly the subject has changed from this shitty town and its mountain to this scrawny naked boy in this shitty little apartment with overhead lights glaring down and a towel around his shoulders.

Time is coming in gasps a little, which is cool, but it's a harsh differential, coming out of the humid and smoky bathroom into the cold dry room with the clear air. Like, his lungs feel relieved and stuff but it feels kind of bad in his brain, in his eyes.

James probably hates his apartment. Like the bathtub was a warm safe womb and now he's suddenly in this horrific bright world. He doesn't scream like a baby taking its first breath, though. He mopes around like the teenager he was until three months ago. The plates next to his computer with pizza bones and toast crumbs on them are depressing. So are the high white walls with nothing on them and the blue futon with the navy blue sheets tangled in a corner. He doesn't make the bed. He rarely even really untangles the sheets before sleeping in them. He lives in a one-room apartment where the kitchen corner is so small that you can't even fit a plate in the sink to leave it there to soak. He doesn't even have a lamp. The whole thing is lit like a cubicle, just the stupid overhead light with the fancy eco lightbulb that was here when he moved in.

James has never actually seen a cubicle except in movies.

He pulls a pair of boxers from the dresser he's had since he was a little kid, this blocky wooden thing that he moved out of his mom's house when he graduated high school and moved into his own place. It looks awkward against the wall in the corner. There are all these burn marks where he's set down pipes or let joints burn out on it. After the first couple times he burned it he decided, Fuck it, part of my childhood or not this piece of furniture is not going to have any real resale value, and if I start thinking about sentimental value I'm just going to lose my shit about everything everywhere anyway so I might as well just not give a fuck and keep burning it. So any more, like, he will just put a joint on it without an ashtray or anything. What's one more burn mark. It's not like this giant block of wood is going to catch on fire.

He thinks about brushing his hair. He thinks about Marsha Brady, Rachel from friends, Zooey Deschanel, but he doesn't even know where the brush is and he probably didn't even wash his hair.

Dave Grohl. Robert Plant.

He doesn't need to put on any more clothes. It's late and it's warm enough not to need a shirt. He catches a glimpse of himself in the smallish mirror on the wall and tries to imagine that he has abs instead of a Shaggy from *Scooby-Doo* scrawny fucking stoner non-abdomen, but it doesn't work. He has no idea what he looks like.

If he goes to sleep now with wet hair he'll wake up with a snake's nest of curly fucked up tangles and weird waves. Plus it's not even midnight yet. It doesn't matter that he has to work at eight in the morning, he can never get to sleep before one or two, so he sits down at the computer. He pushes aside the box from the pizza he ate with Nicole tonight and sits in the computer chair, another hand-me-down from his mom's house. It's a round-backed nice wooden thing that clearly looks like it should be at a respectable kitchen table, all scrollwork or whatever, and it looks pretty out of place in this shitty bachelor apartment that's laid out so spartanly for a computer, movies, and sleeping.

He wakes up his computer and types in his password. As if this shitty night was ever going to end any other way.

4.

Nicole is aware that her boyfriend is kind of strange. Not even strange exactly, but distant, or not all the way present, or something. Obviously part of that is how much weed he smokes. James has a literal subscription to High Times. But it seems like it goes deeper than that, like it's just who he is even underneath the dazed stoner facade.

He's always been a space cadet like that, even when they were little. Nicole has been with James for a long time now, but they certainly did not have a childhood lifelong love affair. She had crushes when she was little, signs that she'd grow up to be the sex maniac she's grown up to be, but never, ever one on little James Hanson. He was the weird, dirty kid playing by himself at the edge of the playground while the other kids played sports and house. The joke about James in third grade was that he ate his own boogers. The joke in fifth grade—kind of weird, in retrospect—was that he slept in a bed *made* out of his own boogers.

She didn't ask him out because he'd changed. He's still exactly the same little kid he always was, drinking by himself at a party, inspiring rumors that he's gay. Nicole started dating him because she changed. When she was fourteen or fifteen she bought a copy of Bitch magazine at Thanks Books at the base of the mountain on the east side and it was all downhill: classic feminist awakening stuff. Dots started connecting. The righteous fury about having to wear a dress to church when she was little and not being allowed to climb trees with the boys came back with the fury of a thousand suns. Turned out she was right to be mad about the way every grown man in town looked at her starting when she was twelve.

She was the sixteen-year-old talking about Andrea Dworkin at the lunch table. Suddenly it made sense to fantasize about making out with Jason Sanger, the floppy-haired second-string kicker on the football team, and then knocking him over instead of marrying him. Basically she could see through misogynist rape culture and didn't want anything to do with it. She tried to be a lesbian, but it didn't work. She would try to think about Kathleen Hanna or Princess Leia or Scarlett Johanson when she jacked off but no luck. At the last second they'd turn into Jason Sanger and his arms, his legs, his smirk and his tiny little butt.

It was a major dilemma until one day, at the lunch table, humorless feminist nonfiction tome on the table in front of her, she noticed James for the first time. Like, noticed noticed. Hair to his shoulders, probably too skinny, almost pretty but carrying himself like a boy, sitting at a table with Mark Richardson, probably talking about weed. James smiled about something. His mouth was probably too big for his head, and this feeling just hit her: That is the kind of boy I need to date. Taller than me but skinny, a boy but not a man, a space cadet instead of an athlete. Somebody who'd listen to her and not try to shut her up.

Those were pretty big assumptions, but Nicole is really smart and she was totally right. She asked him out two days later. She made him a mix tape. Not even on a CD, either, a proper mix tape she made on a boom box. She collaged together a cover and was super intentional about not really including love songs or anything, just the kinds of music that she imagined a cute stoner would like. Long songs, songs where the guitars sound weird, stuff with guitar solos. Suave as hell! But he agreed, even though he looked terrified at first. Nicole has a car so they went to the truckstop out on route 80.

He was checked out from the start, pretty much. He just seemed bewildered, although he did ask to listen to the tape she made him while they were driving. But he didn't try to kiss her or anything, which kind of made her want him to. She knew that was kind of gross but it's how she ended up in his lap in the passenger seat of her own car at eleven PM, November 3rd, two years ago, in the dark far corner of the truckstop parking lot. She's pretty small but it was still pretty uncomfortable and she managed to stop herself from asking him to go fuck her somewhere. Sex-positive feminist or not, she was a seventeen-year-old virgin and not interested in fucking someone before she even knew his middle name. So they made out for a long time but she kept her tights on and then she dropped him off at his parents' house and they've been dating ever since.

And he's weird. She knows that. Mostly he just likes to watch movies and smoke weed. She smokes with him sometimes, but she's not as into it as him. She took mushrooms once. Whatever. He likes to smoke. He smokes enough that you can't really tell he's stoned when he's stoned. He just acts normal. Of course, maybe he's just always high and nobody knows what normal for James Hanson even looks like. So: he smokes and they watch movies, eat food, go to work—he works at Wal-Mart too—and do whatever else it is that weirdo teenagers who just turned twenty do. Once they spent a weekend in Reno.

Sometimes, like tonight, they fight. Sometimes she just want to burn his face down because of how checked out he is, and it makes her want to push him, force him to make a decision. Any decision. Like, she knows that he has really strong opinions about movies, but not because he'd ever tell her about them. Mostly she knows because sometimes he writes about them on his blog. But just now he wouldn't do it, he was like, Let's watch a movie, but then he refused to even vote on anything. So she was like, fine. To be an asshole she was like, Let's watch that movie Drew Carey made a couple years ago. He didn't even say anything to that, so they ended up watching Drew Carey's stupid movie. It was like a contest of wills they were having without acknowledging it. Who would get so mad that this movie was so dumb that they would turn it off and pick something good? She was like, It's not going to be me, but with his Zen ability to disappear, it wasn't going to be him. How can you be so disinterested but so willful at the same time? Weird shit, James.

Plus the movie wasn't even that bad. Nicole's bar for awful is pretty low: no sexual assault and no overt sexism, but it doesn't even need to pass the Bechdel test. But most movies still can't even manage that. Somebody always has to make a fat joke or laugh at a girl who isn't conventionally attractive. But that stuff didn't even happen! Much. By the end of the movie she was like, Well shit, I guess I don't even hate Drew Carey. And if she's going to be honest, she was even more pissed at James than she was before they started watching it. He managed to stay awake, at least, but at the end of the movie she all but blurted, like, What the fuck, dude, now what are we going to do?

She knows she was being a brat, but after sitting there stewing for an hour and forty minutes, she couldn't just let it go. She wanted to have sex and to have that sex make her feel better, and make him feel better, and bring them closer together, and reset stuff, the way sex is supposed to do. Whatever. She knew it was dumb but she took her jeans off and climbed on his lap. He got mad and pushed her off, so she pulled them on and left without saying anything. Waited for him to say something while she rounded up her flannel, her purse, her keys, the half-empty two-liter of Coke. Drawing out her silent exit as long as she could. Stupid. Whatever. It's fine, they fight about stuff sometimes. It's better to let it out, right? She'd rather fight about it than seethe forever. So she came home and he hadn't called. She's definitely not going to call him tonight. Fuck him. She'll hear from him by the weekend and they'll make up. Meanwhile she's going to work on this zine she's been hacking away at for literally like a year. You're not supposed to take home stripped magazines from Wal-Mart, but she sneaks out a huge stack of them almost every week. She collages the shit out of them. It wasn't even supposed to be a very long zine, but it keeps getting longer and longer and longer because she keeps having more and more and more to add to it. It's going to end up being like sixty-four pages.

5.

It's not like James is proud of the porn that he looks at, but what are you supposed to do? Will yourself not to be a pervert? He's tried. He's still trying. He tries most nights.

The only light in the room right now is the light of the computer monitor, the blue and black light of the naked bodies on the screen. He knows how this is going to end, though. He's going to try to watch men fuck women for about half an hour, get depressed, not be able to even get hard, and then look at blogs of pictures of women with captions that turn the pictures into weird and absurd erotic transvestite scenarios.

There are basically four scenarios.

One blog is devoted entirely to quote unquote Scientific Transformations, so like, it will be a picture of a pretty girl in a space station with a caption that reads, Professor MacMillan stepped out of the body regenerator and his assistant smirked at the error. Or whatever. Like the premise is always nanorobots, or body switching machines, or like, who even knows? Gender-change rayguns. There are just all these pictures of women with captions explaining that they used to be men. It's stupid that these are supposed to be, like, scientific, because obviously science that can turn you into Pamela Anderson isn't science anyone is working on. There are archives of these things that go way back into the history of the Internet but that shit is not science, it is fucking magic.

Then there are ones that are explicitly devoted to magic. Like, there will be a picture of a pretty girl in a forest and a caption reading, The evil ice sorceress had turned Brave Samson into a demure maiden. In the erotic minds of the people who make this creeper porn, magic and science are the same thing and mostly what they do is turn men into conventionally attractive women.

There are also angry girlfriend captions. These are the ones where girlfriends make their boyfriends into women for some reason. These ones at least take place kind of in the real world, but it's not like putting lipstick and a dress on the average clueless stoner boyfriend will make him look like the beautiful women who are inevitably pictured.

Stupid.

There are also hardcore ones that barely even have captions, like a picture of a pretty girl sucking some dude's dick and it says, like, Suck it, boy, or whatever. You can't help but wonder who makes these, who is sitting at their computer finding still pictures of blowjobs to write stilted half-sentences on, in order to enable legions of perverts to come all over their computer keyboards? This is a dangerous path of thinking to go down, though, because who the fuck even looks at any of this stuff? It is all so weird and stupid. And at the same time, once you have a boner from looking at this ridiculous shit, suddenly it doesn't seem weird as much as it seems magic. Potent. Fascinating. Magical! Scientific! It's like, this is no longer a dumb picture from a fashion magazine or a porn shoot or a Halloween costume advertisement, subtitled with a stupid scenario. Suddenly this shit is functioning in your reptile brain the way that pussy is supposed to function.

James isn't gay or anything. He's not that into the ones where there are dicks. The ones with lesbians, sure, but he's not into dudes or anything. Like, being a pervert would probably even be easier if he was gay, right, and didn't have to worry about liking girls just in a totally impossible way. Like, there's lots of gay guys, right? If you're a gay guy, you can just go suck a dick in a bathroom at a truck stop or whatever gay guys do. If you're a straight guy who's into the idea of being turned into a girl there's not a lot of girls who are interested in being involved in that, probably. Well there are a lot of imaginary girls who are into that on the Internet, but they're just wish fulfillment, dudes making the worlds they wish they lived in and putting them online. Like World of Warcraft.

It's supposed to be called autogynephilia. It's like a thing. That's the name of the fetish. If it's a fetish? James doesn't know what it is. Being sexually attracted to oneself as female. Hot! Who wouldn't be hot for that?

Gross.

It's the sort of thing you can never tell anyone. A secret you carry with you like an albatross stapled to your neck that you take with you to your grave.

Lots of other fetishes or whatever, like, you can frame them as cool. People can look cool getting tied up and whipped. People can look cool pissing on each other, even. Imagine if Nine Inch Nails put that in a video. You could make that cool. But wanting to be a girl? Not even like, I have known my whole life, man trapped in the body of a woman, whatever. Anyone can tell you that James is not a woman. James knows who Jennifer Finney Boylan is, and he is no Jennifer Finney Boylan. He's just some fuckin dude who wishes he was allowed to wear dresses.

He's looking at a picture of a girl in a French maid Halloween costume: *Philip's girlfriend was furious! It seems he couldn't be bothered to get a costume for her big party so she got one for him—and it was a dress!* It's absurd and he can't even focus on it. He's a million miles away, imagining how ridiculous he would look in that dress, working out scenarios for ways that he could ever connect with another human being about this stuff. There aren't even support groups for transvestites. There are social clubs, which are probably full of hairy men in pantyhose. And James is sure there isn't even a transvestite social club anywhere near Star City. Plus, he has never even worn women's clothes before. What is he going to do, show up to the support group in jeans and a denim jacket and ask to borrow something from someone? There aren't autogynephile support groups, either, because autogynephiles are a kind of transsexual. Sort of. Fake transsexuals: ugly transsexuals. Men who decide to become women even though they're nothing like women. James has looked it up. Kenneth Zucker, J. Michael Bailey. It's science.

He can't even get hard. He should be thinking about himself with Nicole, but he's thinking about himself with his traitorous dick. But he can't even do that right. What kind of twenty-year-old guy has trouble getting hard while he's looking at the kind of porn he likes? What kind of twenty-year-old guy has a lot of trouble coming unless his girlfriend is sucking his dick so he can think about the evil ice sorceress turning Brave Samson into a demure maiden?

6.

It's not one hundred percent true that he's never worn women's clothes.

All through high school, probably somewhere back in the mists of time even before high school, god knows when it showed up, he had this idea. He knew he wasn't going to go to college. He's pretty dumb and barely graduated high school, so his Future has always basically been at best rising through the ranks at Wal-Mart to become a manager and then to die of a corporate heart attack at age fifty. He was never going to move to New York and become a rapper. He has a blog about film that he took seriously for a minute, but nobody cares what he has to say and to be honest he hasn't updated it with anything substantial for like six months because he keeps watching these stupid movies with Nicole that he doesn't care about. The point is, all through high school he could not wait until he could graduate and get his own apartment, where he could have a closet full of dresses.

Whatever the fuck is wrong with him, it isn't that he's a transvestite. He has no idea how to wear a dress. But when he had his own apartment, everything would change. He thought he'd be able to order dresses off the Internet, and then have them in his apartment and wear them whenever he wanted. He started working at Wal-Mart when he was sixteen because he knew it would take a minute to get promoted and start making more than minimum wage. He was going to need to be able to afford not to have a roommate, so he wouldn't even have to just dress up in his room. He was going to invest in really thick curtains, a bunch of mirrors, and then this phenomenal wardrobe: all the most absurd, frilly and short and sexy and demure dresses. And then he could wear them all the time, then figure out what to do from there. Like, not transition. After all, most women in the real world don't even wear dresses much. He wasn't transsexual. He just wanted dresses.

It was a vague plan.

Then life got in the way. Isn't that what you're supposed to say when you're super old, not when you're twenty? It did, though. First, Nicole asked him out, and he didn't have a good reason to say no. Plus he likes her. Plus, having a girlfriend wasn't that far off from having a bunch of dresses. Nicole never really wears skirts any more, even when he tries to hint that it would be cool if she did. She's more of a brown sweater tight jeans hipster glasses and pixie haircut type than a pinup fifties dress lingerie type. And at first it wasn't even complicated. Her ass in his lap got him all hard and he was like Oh, maybe this autogynephilia stuff was just kid stuff and now I can be a Man. Which actually felt kind of gross.

On top of that, how the fuck do you get dresses? You can't just go online and order a dress. You have to know what size you are. You have to measure yourself. But how do you measure yourself? You can't just buy a measuring tape at the Wal-Mart where you work: somebody would notice and ask what you were going to do with it. And a metal tape measure from the tools department doesn't work. James tried. And then even if you just guess that you probably wear a size large, you might have the most depressing experience in the world when you try to test out that theory.

He ordered one. There is a dress in the back of James's closet that nobody has ever noticed before. Why would anyone go into his closet? It seems inevitable that Nicole is going to go looking for a belt to borrow or something, and find it, and James is not going to have an explanation for why a dress that not only can he not fit into, but also one that would have to be about a foot longer, is hung up behind his two suit jackets and single pair of khaki pants.

The first week that he had this apartment, he ordered this dress online. He was like, Freedom! I can finally order myself My First Dress! He ordered it from eBay. The idea was that he was being responsible. It isn't slutty, it isn't pink, and it's not even supposed to be short. It's navy blue with white piping, and he spent the week after he ordered it, which was in the middle of the night a cold sweat click of the Buy Now button, panicking that it was going to be shipped in a box labeled 'dress' and left out in front of the door of his apartment. It wasn't though. Just a plain brown box in front of his door after work one day.

He took it inside breathing shallow little breaths and tried to cut it open. His hands didn't work. Then a fork worked okay to poke through the tape and start some tearing, but he had to find the sharp knife to cut all the tape open. Then the box was on his kitchen counter, next to the plates with the crusts of pizza and grease on them, open like a present, and it wasn't even scary, it was already sad. First of all, he should have hidden the box until after Nicole had come over that night and then left. She was on her way over any minute. Second of all, you could tell immediately that this wasn't the dress he thought he'd ordered. That dress was in his head. The dress in his head was cute, and made him look like he had a waist. It was cool, sort of a hipster Jackie O thing. This dress in the real world, though, was clearly someone's dead grandmother's church dress. It was boxy and square, a thick almost terrycloth kind of fabric. The piping wasn't cool, it was stupid. He didn't even take it out of the box, he just closed the box and buried it under a couple of old Converse boxes in the back of his closet and walked over to the computer. Sat down. Looked at some pervert stuff until Nicole came over. She even knew something was wrong when she got there.

She was like, Are you okay, you're breathing really fast and you look like you're going to cry.

Nah, he said. Nah I just read something really messed up. About baby seals.

Fucking ridiculous.

After she came over that night, and after they had sex, and then after she went home, he did try it on. It looked like a skirt and a jacket, but it was actually only one piece, a dress. Maybe because he'd already come once that night, or because the dress was so ugly and stupid, or maybe because his ribs were all full of disappointment and helium, whatever it was, he didn't even get turned on when he tried it on. He had expected to. The whole point of actually getting his first dress was to satisfy this impulse that was supposed to be all sexual.

He didn't have a full-length mirror or anything, but he could barely figure out how to get his shoulders into it, and then it tangled around his ribs and armpits and he was worrying that he was going to stretch it out and ruin it—wouldn't it be a tragedy, to ruin such a beautiful thing—but eventually he got into it and felt probably dumber than he had ever felt. There was tons of room and drape in the hips. His stomach, even though it barely even exists, bulged out against the front of the dress. He realized that he hadn't known what he'd expected to feel when he tried this dress on, but it certainly wasn't this emptiness verging on boredom butting up against wanting to die.

But he had it and this was what he'd wanted so he checked to make sure the front door was locked, then checked to make sure the side door was locked, closed all the blinds, and smoked the rest of the weed that he had, sitting on the futon in that stupid dress, feeling like an idiot. And then even when he was really, really high, he didn't stop feeling stupid. He tried to jack off and it didn't work.

This is how James knows he's an autogynephiliac instead of a transvestite. Cross-dressing seems exciting in theory but in practice it is the saddest and most disappointing thing in the world.

That should have been the end of his career as a transvestite, but the next night Nicole was doing something else, who knows what, so he didn't jack off all day and then he tried the dress on again at like eleven o'clock and managed to come that time, but it felt even worse than jacking off while reading stupid Internet caption porn. Like, he came, but there was barely an orgasm, and there was no euphoria, and then he was just like, What the hell. Am I not a transvestite? Do I not like dresses? Do I have a fetish that you can't even do in real life, like being turned on by being eaten by slutty giants?

He couldn't make sense of it, so he buried that dress in the back of his closet for good. He didn't throw it out, because it would be even worse to throw it out, and maybe somehow the situation could be salvaged. Doubtful, considering how much he hated this dress, but he still couldn't bring himself to get rid of it.

The same melancholy and depressing feeling that characterized the whole dress incident culminated in this feeling that he couldn't ball it up and throw it under a bunch of stuff in the back of his closet, so he hung it up. Even though he hated that dress, he liked the idea of having it hanging back there in his closet. Autogynephilia, man.

7.

James is sitting in the dark, trying to get as stoned as he can, dick in one hand, then bong in both, then his dick in one and then the bong again, spacing out and thinking about this dress in his closet that he hates, this girl that he's supposed to love but doesn't really feel anything about. Thinking, What the fuck is wrong with you, dude. Shit like that. If he were in a French movie maybe he'd put his dick away and go for a late night walk where he would feel feelings, but dude a late night walk in Star City looks like fucking nothing. He'd walk by a bunch of houses either to Wal-Mart or to the highway access road or the desert. And anyway, this is an American film. If it were a Tarantino movie maybe he'd kill everybody. In a David Lynch movie it wouldn't even be clear what happened next but you would know it was something. But obviously this isn't a movie and he's just a stupid clueless pervert stoner with no idea what the fuck is going on in his life.

Maybe he should call Nicole. He doesn't even understand that fight they had. He didn't want to have sex so now they are having a fight? You were supposed to be allowed to say no to sex. That was what sex positive feminism was about: choice. Isn't consent important? But maybe he did it wrong, or maybe that's just for women. Whatever. They've had this fight before and it didn't go anywhere then and he's sure they'll have it again. She'll come over tomorrow night and he'll be like, I dunno. And she'll be like, I dunno. And then one of them will apologize and then the other will apologize and they'll go back to pissing their lives away with shitty Drew Carey movies forever.

Eventually he gets stoned enough that he gets off, comes into a sock he's already worn twice, and is able to go to sleep.

8.

As soon as Maria Griffiths sees James Hanson in the Star City, Nevada Wal-Mart she's like, That kid is trans and he doesn't even know it yet.

9.

He smokes out before he gets to work, but by hour four or so of a nine hour shift he's not really feeling stoned any more. Every day by this point he mostly feels tired and pissed off. He's always wished he could be the kind of cool badass who smokes out at work, but there's no way you could do it without somebody finding out. Plus his mom rides in his car sometimes, so he can't even hotbox it ever. It's actually very possible that this is why he hates his job so much. He's like, I should think about that more. Every single day I go through an unstoned-ening and fucking hate my life and my job and my house and my girlfriend and everyone and everything that I can see. It seems like that probably affects my job satisfaction. I end each shift with a headache. I need a fix, man, because I am addicted to the she-demon marijuana.

It is getting toward the end of his shift and James isn't stoned any more and it sucks. This old guy who comes in once or twice a week was looking for some stupid old movies that he couldn't find because Wal-Mart doesn't carry stupid old movies but this guy doesn't listen to James at all, so they always wind up spending half an hour pretending to look for these DVDs that aren't there.

That's probably a metaphor for life in Star City, actually. Whatever. Once or twice a week James thinks very seriously about writing out a note to have waiting for this guy the next time he comes in that explains that these are very, very old and hokey movies, starring actors that nobody cares about any more, and that he'd be better off going to the Family Dollar over in Imlay where they sell those mass-produced DVDs of public domain stuff that feel all light in your hands like there's no DVD in them.

Wal-Mart can't even order them. Those DVD companies have their own distributors that Wal-Mart doesn't use. Which is weird, since it seems like the distributors that make those wholesome DVDs would be Christian, and Wal-Mart doesn't shy away from Christian anything. But whatever. Who cares. James has a headache, he needs to smoke out again, and this old guy is starting to seem done with playing out this scenario yet again, when Maria Griffiths comes strutting up the aisle of the Wal-Mart looking out of place as hell, like she's made of long red hair and layers of clothing.

James does what anybody would do when they see somebody they'd like to know: he ignores the shit out of her. Probably he freaks out a little. But she came right to the music and movies section, so what else could he do? He says hi to her when she first comes in because he can get in trouble if he doesn't. According to Wal-Mart corporate policy, greetings turn thieves into friends. But then he just ignores her like hell. Maybe on some level he notices that she might have looked at him for a second longer than was appropriate, but if he half-thinks anything it's like, Suck it up, dude, that girl is definitely not checking you out.

She is wearing more clothes than he's ever seen anyone wear at once: huge black boots, a long black skirt or maybe a dress, what looks like a shorter, dark orangey skirt on top of it, a long maroonish sweater under a ratty denim jacket with a bunch of patches and buttons on it, a black scarf, and wavy, dried-out-looking hair down just past her shoulders. Her hair is almost exactly the same color as her sweater, but a little bit darker. They probably clash or whatever. Her clothes look like she slept in them. There are permanent-looking crinkles in the elbows of her jacket and her hair looks like it would leave a mark if she leaned her head against a wall. She looks like she is probably a rock star or a murderer. One time the band Creed came to his Wal-Mart on tour to buy batteries or something and everybody flipped out even though Creed is a stupid band, but James saw one of the guys from the band and he walked with this magnetism or swagger or something, like he knew he was a big deal, and Maria carries herself kind of the same way.

She walks over to the pop/rock CD display and James thinks clearly, who the fuck wears a scarf in the daytime in Star City, especially during a heatwave? While he's ignoring her he stares at her back. Steven Tyler? The fourth Doctor? He is seriously just being a creep and staring at her because people who look like that don't live here. They don't stop here while they're driving through, either. There are other Wal-Marts close to the highway. Like, three exits away in either direction on route 80. It was fucking dumb for Wal-Mart to put a Wal-Mart here. Well. Nobody comes here except for Creed. Once.

She flips through the pop/rock cds for a second and James manages to look away from the Poison patch safety-pinned across her back and the messy wavy hair sprawling its way down it. Like, Poison, the ridiculous glam rock band with the singer who does reality TV shows now? His headache fades or else James just forgets about it because when she turns around he is very intently alphabetizing cds that have just come in and need to be shelved.

Hey, she says, looking him up and down again.

James is like, Hi.

Do you have the Miranda Lambert album?

Um, he says, Probably, but it's probably in the country section.

She's like Oh, there's a country section?

And he says, Well, yeah.

Then, because he's feeling totally weird, James doesn't even stop himself, he just blurts out, You don't look like the folks who usually shop there, though.

Because if he's being totally honest with himself, on some level James has already figured out that this girl is trans and while he hasn't processed what that means yet he is having this desperate magnetic attraction to her. Like not even sexual. Just like, I want to be your Facebook friend or something. I need to grab you, to have you in my life. Whatever.

You don't look like the folks who usually shop here, that's a pretty dumb thing to say, but she doesn't disagree.

She looks at his name tag, smirks, and says, That's probably true, James H., but check this out. I left New York City about a week ago and my dog, my cat and I have been living out of my car since then, driving out to the West Coast solely because we've never seen it. In New York City, there are Spanish music stations, rap stations, dumb rock stations, and little stations run by painfully self-aware college students with no idea what to do with all their privilege besides collect records and gentrify neighborhoods that have been fine for generations. But I don't think there's a country station in New York. I guess there are a lot of reggaeton stations, which in a lot of ways people tend to not even notice has a lot of similarities to country music. Anyway it turns out, though, that once you leave New York, which nobody should ever do, haha, j/k, the only things you can consistently get on a twelve year old car stereo are NPR and country stations. And have you ever listened to NPR? It's soothing for a while, but eventually it makes you want to call in and cuss somebody out until you cry. It wouldn't get onto the radio, because I guess they have enough lag time to dump out angry people who call up and lose their shit, but it turned me off NPR for a while. Which means country station after country station for the last four days. And I'm not some New York jerk who thinks country music is for yokels or something—I'm into it, I get it. I even think it's kind of nice that country singers are so fucking convinced of their own sincerity that they don't do any of the tortured artist, I don't care if you like me it's art, man posturing that all the indie rock kids do. And they don't spend all day telling me about how tough and rich they are, like the rappers on the radio do. Except, James H., there is also a lot of dumb shit on country radio. 'I'm so much cooler online?' 'She thinks my tractor's sexy?' I guess it's funny the first time. But! But!

Maria has followed James over to the country music section and is jabbing her pointer finger toward his chest.

I guess, she says, Miranda Lambert isn't the biggest star in the country sky, because I've only heard the radio play her a couple times. But I think all her songs are about burning down cheating ex-boyfriends' houses and, like, shooting your abusive ex in the face? The first time I heard *that* song I was like, Finally! Someone is just coming out and threatening to kill her asshole boyfriend, right there on the radio! Not that I think anybody should kill anybody else or anything, but after five days of country radio, consider me brainwashed. Miranda Lambert, James H., is the punkest shit on the radio, and I am going to drive my car off a cliff if I hear the song about how the guy hopes he gets a chance to live like he was dying. Ever again. Not because I don't like it though—because it's so sad and true that it makes me want to live like I was dying and then, like, die. So, James H., Miranda Lambert is a contingency plan to save my life.

Then she actually said the Internet abbreviation for just kidding out loud.

There's a pause and then she smirks and she's like, Sorry, I guess I haven't really talked to anybody in a while.

James is like, It's cool. He picks Miranda Lambert's second album out and hands it to her.

This is the CD with that song about the gunpowder and lead on it, he says.

Thank you, James H., she says. You've been very helpful.

Then she starts to leave the movies and cds department.

Wait, James says, You've got to buy it here, or else security will kick my ass.

This is kind of true. Mostly true, you're supposed to get people to buy their music and DVDs in the music and DVDs section, even though there isn't like a rule about it or anything. It's a firm suggestion in the interest of loss prevention. But it's a stupid thing to emphasize just then. It's not like he's going to slip her his phone number on the receipt.

Well. The receipt does have the phone number for Wal-Mart #8304 on it, if she wants to call him.

I don't think they could take you, she says. You look like a total bruiser.

Yeah, he says. Totally. I'm a regular ol' Brad Paisley.

Which one is Brad Paisley?

Y'know, he says, I don't highlight my hair, and I've still got a pair?

Maria's eyes light up and she quotes from this dumb country song: My eyebrows ain't plucked and there's a gun in my truck!

That's me, he says, Honey, I'm still a guy. It's ten dollars and ninety cents.

The weirdness of that exchange isn't lost on either of them.

Maria pays with a debit card. James notices that her PIN is 6664. Then she leaves and he thinks, well fuck. Then his headache is back and he gets pretty bummed so he starts thinking about how, like, soon he is going to go home and get high as fuck.

Smoking weed rules and the fact that this girl just showed up in his life and now she is gone forever totally sucks. He's thinking about this weird girl who was just here whose name he doesn't even know because she paid with a PIN instead of credit, and then his thoughts naturally and optimistically turn toward his go-to non-sexual fantasy: weed.

He's envisioning like laying down in the sprawling fields of the marijuana farms of Northern California but she keeps stomping in. Even though it is his go-to fantasy, James is aware that it's pretty boring. More interesting things tend to intrude. Like, fantasizing about laying down in a field of weed crops, it's like licking the centerfold of an issue of High Times. He just keeps thinking like, New York City. Her and a dog and a cat in a car for a week, what the fuck is reggaeton... trans!

It's weird that he could tell that she was trans. You could tell. But not in like an obvious way, like if a drag queen came parading up the aisle. You couldn't really tell from the way she looked, or the way she talked, or anything. Probably? But then you have to ask yourself, like, well, how could I tell? It was probably some kind of combination of things. But could other people tell? Was he going to have to have stupid conversations for the next three months with idiot coworkers about the freaky queer that was in the store that one time? Gross. Weird.

10

Because look it's not like James doesn't think about whether he's trans too, right? To be totally honest he thinks about it all the fucking time, he just can't imagine actually being trans in the real world. Does he wish he was a girl? Fucking—obviously he wishes he was a girl. You don't spend twenty-nine hours a week thinking about being a girl and masturbating without wondering, like, I wonder if this pattern is trying to tell me something. And to be honest he probably hasn't committed to it either way. Like there are a million reasons why he obviously is not trans or is not the kind of trans person who transitions. He has never said it out loud or even explicitly thought it but he is probably kind of genderqueer, so he doesn't even know what to think about it. He's looked at a lot of people's websites and blogs and read up on autogynephilia and what hormones do and don't do and he knows that if he's transsexual he's definitely not, like, a normal kind of transsexual, normal transsexuals all fucking know they're transsexual when they're little kids and fucking tell their parents and get yelled at for it or else start hormones when they're thirteen and don't fucking spend every night of their lives jacking off and reading embarrassing as hell pornography that is stupid and boring and repetitive and, like, just an entirely different avenue of gender and sexuality expression so whatever who cares, the point is just, like, James is aware of transsexuality.

Maybe, like, very aware.

So maybe he's on the lookout for it? Of course he's on the lookout for, like, weird gender stuff in everyone all the time or whatever, like he's hypersensitized or something. But he definitely just was like, oh my god, a trans person! But he choked it down and didn't say anything because he is totally good at choking things down and not saying anything. Like, feelings and stuff.

So maybe he is on the lookout for transsexuals all the time and finally he saw one? Whatever man, who knows? Who even knows how to talk about this stuff without being disrespectful so whatever, never mind, the point is just, it took a minute after she left to even put together that that was what had been the thing about her. Except she was gone now, right? He was like, I do have the credit card slip, maybe I could do some kind of hacker shit with it if I was a creep. And if he had the time and energy and focus to learn to do hacker shit. On some level he's been meaning to learn that stuff for a long time. So.

11

Maria doesn't go right back into the Wal-Mart. She walks back out to Steph's car, sits down and turns the key. She hadn't thought to find a tree to park under, so the car is really hot. She's thankful for a second that she hasn't brought cutoffs to wear because if she'd been wearing jorts she would have literally burned the bottoms of her thighs on the hot vinyl. She could probably take off the long skirt she's wearing under the shorter skirt but then she would feel nervous about her junk. The orange skirt isn't sheer, but it's not thick either—and even velvet drapes. So she sits in the car, foot above the gas pedal, the sticky brake pedal, not driving. Waiting for the air conditioning to cool the car down.

The air conditioning in Steph's car isn't great, but it works. The whole car feels like maybe a Platonic solid, if that's a thing. Like, it's sort of old, and sort of busted, but not truly old or busted, and nothing in it is really broken or particularly effective. The air works, but it never really gets cold. It can accelerate, but not so much if it's going uphill.

She's thinking: I should go, let's go. But there's a tug at the telephone wire that connects her heart to her brain. It's more taut than usual. On some level she's thinking, this is what's going on, Maria, this is what you're doing, this is the whole point of this trip you're on right now. This thing. Right here.

She drove almost all the way across the country trying to figure out what the fuck is wrong with her: why she can't be present in a relationship, why she can't keep track of her money. Why she can't even manage to give herself a shot every two weeks. It seems clear that it's something to do with being trans and probably something to do with the way that being trans interrupts normal human development, but instead of getting stuck at the anal stage or whatever, you end up getting stuck at the tween stage, the Nickelodeon stage, the I can take care of myself but I suck at it stage. That's the obvious reason that she flipped out and bought a bunch of drugs that to be honest she is too wimpy to even fuck around with, and then tried to disappear, and it's why she keeps charging her cell phone, reading Steph and Piranha and Kieran's texts and thinking, yeah, tonight, I'll respond to that when I pull over, when I stop to eat I'll definitely let them know that I'm not dead. But not doing it. For the last couple days she's been charging her phone through the cigarette lighter but not turning it on for longer than it takes to reread those texts. Steph's reported the car stolen. Kieran's obnoxious. Piranha misses her blog, which sounds sarcastic.

The central thing here is that Maria is really good at being trans.

Maybe that is just relative to other people, but she has figured this one thing out and she is good at it. The couple hundred people who read her livejournal agree. Trans women are like Wow, you said that so well, and cis people are like Wow, I had never thought about that that way. Maria can explain to you exactly what she's figured out and how she figured it out and can smell cisnormativity from like a hundred yards. She just sucks at pretty much everything else.

Sitting there in a warm car in a Wal-Mart parking lot under a hot sun in the early afternoon she is thinking: I might not know shit about my own life; I've learned a lot from Steph about sex and community and perspective and queerness and all these other really important things, but nothing about what to do when somebody looks at me on the train, or what to do when I can't afford rent and it's the third and I'm not getting paid for another five days and I'm afraid to call my mom and I know that theoretically we've got a community that supports its people but in practice what am I going to do, put a paypal button on my blog? I guess that's no moochier than throwing a top surgery party but right now, at this moment, in this car and without a computer, putting a paypal button on my blog is not going to solve anything. So far this stupid little jaunt away from the center of the universe hasn't taught me anything about how to live a life post-transition and it sure doesn't seem likely that I'm going to get to Oakland or San Francisco, or drive up to Portland, to Seattle or Olympia, and find somebody there who will sit me down and explain what I need to do to exist like a three-dimensional person who cares about her body and her mind and her life and her friends and her lovers and is able to exist in a relationship with another person. How to exist as a person who knows what she's feeling and can express that to another person.

Maria knows people who transitioned years before she did, even a couple people who started transitioning like a decade before she did. They're not fuckups. But they're not, like, buddhas, either. She's thought of them as buddhas, in her life, and then been disappointed when they've explained that their enlightenment consists of the same platitudes that every enlightenment consists of: Fuck what people think, and I dunno man, and There is no center at the center of things. It's like, cool, but then how do you repair the damage that a fucking lifetime of not giving a fuck about your life did to you?

The dashboard looks like it's probably cool enough to touch when she's thinking, fine, there's no epiphany. The only way to be a buddha is just to be a buddha, to disregard the shit that's in the way of being a buddha. So she's like, fine, if enlightenment is just sitting here, in the car with me, on my lap, weightless and violent, then fine, enlightenment. Fine.

Maybe what Maria needs isn't staring at her own navel and getting mad at herself for being useless. Maybe what she needs to do is to look the fuck away from the mirror for twenty minutes and pay attention to someone else: to someone who could actually use what little she does understand, the little wisdom she does have. What she probably should be doing right now is getting the fuck out of this car. It occurs to her that if the dog and the cat she told James H. were in this car hadn't been rhetorical embellishments but had instead been imaginary companions for this whole car ride, maybe she wouldn't feel so outstandingly weird and unproductive right now, maybe she could just have spent a lot of time working this shit out with an imaginary dog and cat, instead of a very real cramped up and tired pointer finger exhausting the scan button on the radio.

The scan button's probably the cleanest surface in this car and she's like, fine, I'm gonna go talk to that girl and tell her that she's a girl and she's going to be like Nah I'm not a girl, and I'm going to be like No, you are a girl, and she's going to be like Yeah the only reason I said I wasn't a girl is that I'm a girl but it seems like it would be impossible to get from this body and social situation to a body that reads as female and friends who read me as female and I'll be like Yeah let's talk about that I have a lot of thoughts on the subject and she's going to be like, cool, and I'm going to be like, Yeah, you're young and you're not that tall and you look like puberty has barely even gotten to your house, let's get you on hormones ASAP and she'll be like I don't know man and we'll talk and she'll cry and I'll set her up a livejournal so she can sort through all her feelings and then I'll leave and totally learn something about myself, too.

She turns the car back off but cracks the window. Then she opens the rest of the windows, too, locks the door and walks back across the parking lot.

12.

Ten minutes after Maria leaves, just as James has made peace with the fact that he's never going to see this girl again, she comes strutting back up the aisle toward him. Maria Motherfucking Griffiths, Queen of All She Surveys. There's an expression on her face that's kind of hard to look at, like she's just about convinced herself that she's cool and in control. But not quite. It's like, you almost can't see that she's terrified.

James H., she says when she gets to the music and movies section. Her voice doesn't sound terrified, I know we don't know each other or anything, but I've been driving for a long time and not really talking to anyone about anything anywhere, for a long time, and now that I've stopped in a proper town, I'm thinking about hanging out for a minute, but I don't know anybody here. Except, like, you? I was kind of hoping you could show me around.

James responds without thinking: This is a fuckin' dumb town to stop in. Then he looks around. That's not the sort of thing you're supposed to say when you're the public representative of the Wal-Mart corporation.

I mean, he says, Uh, look, yeah, I guess so? There isn't really much to show you but I guess I'm not doing anything.

He has this very clear thought that while it's weird for a stranger just to come up and ask you to hang out, especially a stranger who looks like a murderess, that even if she actually is a literal murderess, this is still probably the only chance he's ever going to have to, like, talk to an actual trans woman. His next thought is one long whoa but the one after that is a shapeless thing about how, like obviously she doesn't know about him and whatever his deal with gender is, and obviously he can't let her know that he can tell that she's trans because that would obviously be rude as hell. That this is going to be kind of complicated to navigate or whatever? And then once he's thought all this stuff he ends up at probably the first thing he should have thought, which is like, what would Nicole think about him not seeing her tonight? For one single night out of the entirety of their desolate union or whatever, and on that one day out of like seven hundred or whatever it's been, like sort of going out with this other girl?

So he blurts: Also I have a girlfriend so—

She laughs.

Yeah whatever James H. don't worry, one I don't even date dudes—James winces and tries to hide it—and two I'm probably ten years older than you so we're not even, like, in the same dating league. Technically speaking. Ethically speaking.

Cool, he says. He has an urge to ask for that in writing, thinking whoa, she is into girls! If you read the Internet a little bit you know that there are trans women who are into girls and it's a little bit terrifying to think about because if you can be trans *and* into girls then, like, that makes it more possible that he could even be trans, like legitimately for real trans, which he doesn't even want to think about and obviously that is not even a very compelling argument. That it is a possibility. Who cares. But he's still kind of like, thank you Divine Providence for dropping this hot, weird dyke trans girl into my lap, out of nowhere, in a totally nonsexual manner.

He thinks, maybe me and Nicole are even broken up though. He'd just assumed he'd see her in a day or two and nothing would have happened and they'd be unbroken up again, like what always happens, but now he's like, actually, this matters. And then he realizes wait, shit, I already said it out loud, that I have a girlfriend. Obviously that is the classic defensive maneuver if a girl hits on you: no way man, I have a secret girlfriend! She lives in, um, Olympia! For college. But James was already thinking about Nicole and he doesn't want to date anyone ever so she's a good excuse but also he actually also, like, is in a relationship with her. In real life.

Maria asks when he gets off and instead of making a stupid joke about getting off James is like, I dunno, in like half an hour.

Cool, she says, I'm in this ugly little green car at the far end of the parking lot, there's a bunch of embarrassing bumper stickers and it hasn't been washed in a while.

And there's a dog and a cat.

Haha, yeah, she says. A dog and a cat. Totally.

Half an hour later James clocks out and finds her car right away. It's not like the Star City Wal-Mart parking lot is ever fucking full. She's sitting under a tree in front of the green car, looking all sweaty.

Hey, she says.

Hey.

They look at each other for a second, the entirety of the terror of whatever is about to happen a physical presence in the air between them, before James breaks the tension with the totally suave acknowledgment Uh, aren't you hot?

Yeah dude, she says, But I have this dilemma, right? I'm enough of a feminist not to shave my legs really ever, but not enough of a feminist to actually let anybody see.

But like, you're wearing a sweater and a jacket and stuff.

She waits a beat and then goes, James H., have you ever spent a couple weeks in the same clothes?

He's like, I don't think so, and she goes, You just get kind of used to it and the longer you don't take anything off the less you want to. Like y'know Spider-Man and the Venom suit? Same thing.

James tries to keep up but he's already getting lost. He needs to smoke.

I know... of... Spider-Man and Venom, he says.

So listen, what do people do here? Is there a lake where we can go and drink beer or like a trestle where kids smoke weird shit and burn each other with cigarettes?

Uh, there's a river. But it sucks.

James H., Maria says, I get it. Everything here sucks. But I don't want to drive any further toward the Pacific right now and what else are we going to do. Sit here and hotbox the car?

James is like: Well. Actually.

13.

He does the logistics. If they're going to sit in a car with the windows up, they're going to have to find someplace shady to do it, and someplace away from where the cops would drive by. They will have to be committed to the plan. Basically what this means is that they have to drive back to his apartment building and park in the shade of the eastern side of the building. Which is cool, he's gotten all baked there a bunch of times, nobody cares. It's just like, if they're going to drive all the way over to the house, they might as well hotbox his fucking bathroom.

But she's company so they park in a shady spot behind the apartment building and he smokes her out. It's like she's never smoked out before, she's all coughing and having to take long breaks between tokes and then once she's stoned she can't really communicate right. Her sentences trail off, she starts laughing at nothing. It's kind of annoying, actually. She keeps laughing at the idea of, like, that band Sublime, who are actually not bad. But since she can just barely hold up her end of the conversation, James starts monologuing and after a while she kind of gets into the groove of it, nodding like she's following what he's saying and stuff. Mostly he finds himself talking about Nicole. He's like, here's the thing, I have this girlfriend, and I really like her, she's cool as hell, but. But the fact even that there's a but kind of means something, right? He's like, it's not even that I don't want to be in a relationship with her, I just, I don't want to be in this context, working this job, living in this apartment, in this town, and she's a part of that. He's probably not doing a good job explaining it but he starts envisioning My Life and Everything as this huge, complicated braid, like a friendship bracelet, with the different threads in it representing, like, his job, and Nicole, and his apartment, and his mom, and all the things that end up making up the tapestry of his life. The friendship bracelet of his life. He knows it's a dumb stoner epiphany but he's going for it, he's like, Nicole is one of the strands of that thread, she's tied to this town and this life, and I just, I'm like, I don't know if I can get away from all this stuff I don't care about or want and stay with her, you know?

Maria's like, Did she say that, and James is like, Did she say what, and Maria's like, Y'know, did Nicole say she wanted to stay here?

James thinks about it and has to admit that no, not in so many words, probably not, but he's like, well she's never said anything about wanting to leave, I guess.

Here's the thing, James H., she says, still looking all dazed but suddenly lucid. What do you want?

Not all this, he says.

No I know, Maria says, But what do you want? It's easy to say that where you are and what you have are dumb, but it's harder and probably more productive to name concrete things and aspire to them. You know?

James hasn't even thought about actually wanting things before, so he's like, Jesus, I have no idea what I actually want. Maybe to move to the bay?

Sick dude, she says, picking up the sticky green blown-glass pipe, taking a hit, holding it in, then exhaling: Me too.

James is like Haha oh yeah and she's like Haha, yeah man, and they both laugh. The smoke in the car isn't as thick as a Cheech and Chong movie or anything, but it's pretty intense, everybody's eyes are starting to get watery and painful.

For real though, Maria says, Think about specifics. Do you want to be in a band? Do you want to go to college, write a novel, sit in a tree so that nobody can bulldoze it? Do you want to have lots of weird sex, no sex, lots of weird vegan food, a haircut that reads like a secret code that identifies you as a member of a subculture to other members of that subculture. Be specific, James H., because now is the time in your life when you can do anything. And anything is gonna turn out great.

She's talking weird so James is like, What are you quoting right now, dude.

Old Faith No More, she says.

James has heard of Faith No More.

Listen, do you want to go inside and find some food and stuff, he asks.

Fuck yeah I do, Maria says, do you have frozen pizzas?

I think so, yeah, James says, thinking pretty hard about frozen pizza. Fuck yeah. Finally: something awesome.

14.

Okay Maria didn't mean to get too stoned to have a real talk but like a baked-ass Machiavellian genius, she managed to turn the conversation toward serious stuff right away. Even baked out of her head she could tell right away that this kid's relationship with his girlfriend wasn't the problem. Nicole is probably nineteen and cool and way ahead of James in terms of pretty much everything. James just doesn't know how to be in a relationship because he doesn't know how to be himself and you can't be one of the people in a relationship if you're busily refusing to be a person.

Right?

And his apartment doesn't look like the apartment of a person. It isn't the standard 20-year-old boy apartment though—there's no sink full of dishes, no armpit smell. It's like a nonapartment, a ghost apartment. It's literally, like, an overhead light, a futon, a computer desk, a beat up old little kid's dresser, and a flimsy-looking entertainment center with an enormous old 27-inch tube television. There are ways you could tell it was a Young Dude's apartment: speakers so large they look out of place, hooked up to the stereo that gleams more brightly than anything else in the room. The extensive and neatly arranged library of DVD cases. It's all, like, Classic Films, too, instead of complete anime series or something.Pretentious, fully enmeshed in patriarchal systems of validity determination, but at least not weird and annoying.

It takes her a second to figure out why a space so sparsely populated with stuff could feel lived in at all. It hits her: it's because everything is saturated in weed smoke. The dust on the TV screen and the DVD shelves is clearly as least as much ash and THC as it is old skin and the dust mites who love it. It's seeped deep into every surface.

There's no pizza.

Can we order in, Maria asks.

I dunno man. I guess. I mean, there's a Domino's, but that shit sucks and it's expensive. There's a spot by the Wal-Mart but I guess I'm kind of avoiding it.

James doesn't mention that he's avoiding it because he's avoiding his girlfriend. He hasn't really acknowledged this to himself.

15

They eat some frozen tater tots and then Maria just, like, hangs out. This is probably James's first clue that this girl isn't going to give him the adventure in personal growth, or at least the cool story, that he was sort of hoping for. It actually gets kind of uncomfortable: he keeps smoking even though she stops and then he's like, well, I guess maybe we could watch a movie? She's like, yeah, cool, and falls asleep upright on the futon pretty much as soon as he puts on whatever it was he put on. Twin Peaks or something. Then he's like, fuck man, now what do I do? He sits down at his computer like, I wish I knew if she was a heavy enough sleeper that I could jack off.

Not really an appropriate thought.

But it starts to occur to him that this Girl From Somewhere Else isn't going to show him what it means to be cool, or explain the secret of getting out of your shitty home town, or involve him in some mysterious occult ritual under the glare of the half moon or something. He probably should have just called Nicole. It's like eight o'clock and he hasn't even texted her so he digs out his phone.

Three new texts. Fuck.

They're all from Nicole, increasing in forced nonchalance:

hey james what are you doing?

hellooooo

okay im making a mix tape nbd

He texts her back like, Hey im actually feeling kinda shitty, fell asleep after work, see you tomorrow?

She texts back right away: cool

He knows on some level that he's being a stoner asshole but every syllable in those exchanges made him feel like the world was ending. What's up anxiety. Fuck. He packs another bowl and smokes it. Stares at the computer. You can't see the computer monitor from the futon and Maria is sleeping like she's dead, but she's definitely breathing so James looks at sleazy porn captions for a while without masturbating, lurks at a message board for an hour without absorbing anything, looks up a half-remembered Nickelodeon show from when he was little, puts in an ear bud and goes down a youtube rabbit hole of videos about transitioning, looks up and sees that it's past midnight. Maria hasn't moved, she's like a garbage bag full of wet leaves on his futon. So James is like Oh, I guess you're sleeping over, hunts down his sleeping bag in the back of his closet, and goes to sleep on the floor across the room from her.

He goes to sleep thinking about the last thing he googled before locking up the computer, 'how do you politely ask if someone is trans?'

Pretty much everybody agrees that there isn't a polite way to do it. But what else is he going to do? He smokes once more before bed but he can't stop worrying about it. He kind of needs to talk to her about it.

Worrying when you're stoned is the worst.

The next morning he just asks her, though. She's laying there like in that way where you can tell she's awake, she just doesn't know what to do with herself, like rolling over and sighing and probably she has to pee but didn't want to wake him up by getting up. A classic politeness stalemate. James tries to roll over really loud but she doesn't look over. He coughs and fakes a sneeze, checks the time on his phone. It's early, but she's just lying there so James is like, okay, fuck it, and starts packing a bowl. He's pretty quiet about it but she must decide that that's enough movement and noise because she's like, Oh hey.

James is like, Oh hey.

He tries not to notice that her face has, like, stubble.

So uh, he says, staring deep into the bowl of the pipe like he's going to find something in it, breaking up a nug and trying to look like he wasn't asking something inappropriate, You're trans right?

Fuck, she mutters. She gets up off the futon, walks over to the bathroom and closes the door behind her.

16.

Maria, in the bathroom, is thinking, Dude just straightup asked if I was trans! That might not ever have happened to me before. When she was first transitioning, people would give her shit on the train and stare at her and she heard a lot of That's a dude and You a fuckin man, but in James H.'s little bathroom with the water faucet that felt like you could snap it off by accident she's thinking, Is that even rude?

Like, it had been her plan since yesterday to tell him she was trans so she could talk about it and they could get him to stare down his own trans stuff. And it should be a value-neutral question, isn't it? In a world that was less fucked up about trans people, it would be a perfectly legitimate question: maybe kind of rude, like do you dye your grey hair or something. But in this world that question was making her hyperventilate.

She intentionally takes some long slow breaths, splashes some water on her face, decides that she won't smoke any weed today no matter how politely this kid offers it to her—no matter how innocent and tired his face looks when he asks—and pushes down the panicked, angry, anguished, and affronted thing that had risen up her chest into her throat. She looks at her sleepy face in the mirror, yesterday's mascara smudged under her eyes, a futon crease up one cheek: James H. is allowed to ask if you're trans, stupid. That's the whole fucking point, Maria! The fact that you're not the one choosing when to disclose is probably for the best anyway since we left it up to you yesterday and all you did was get high and fall asleep.

She's like, okay, I'll just talk about being trans. No big deal. I talk about being trans all the time! Just not out loud. And she thinks, maybe it's been a long enough time since I had to talk about this. Maybe now this conversation doesn't have to be all panicky and sad.

Basically she's like, okay, I can do this. Even though I guess I already decided to do this.

She thinks for a second about shaving and putting on makeup before leaving the bathroom. She actually really wants to; if you're going to be talking about being trans it would've been nice to put on some small show of, like, look how passable you can turn out, look how pretty and poised and together you can grow up to be. Obviously that is a misogynist patriarchal mandate: look pretty! But let's be real about the fact that before transitioning, how many trans women have a good handle on breaking down patriarchal mandates for women? Also, who hasn't internalized that stuff? Stockholm syndrome with patriarchy, it's unavoidable, even when you're resisting it and not shaving your armpits, you have to hear about it from every mook on the subway every day. And when you're a trans woman, patriarchal mandates about presentation get extra twisted up with narratives of disclosure, validity as a human being, violence, the possibility of ever being found attractive, and probably a bunch of other stuff you haven't even identified yet. It makes it actually pretty complicated to leave the bathroom once you're in it. Anyway the whole thing is moot because she left her makeup bag with her razor and stuff out in the car, so she finds a hairbrush and almost runs it through her hair before noticing, in the mirror, that this brush is pretty much bulging in every direction with long, stringy, dishwater brown hairs that she doesn't really want to touch her head. Never mind. She puts the hairbrush down, runs her fingers through the length of her hair a couple times to untangle the knottiest knots, and opens the door.

She sits back down on the futon. At some point she's taken off her longer skirt and it would've been awkward to put it back on right then so she puts a pillow in her lap and she's like, Yes James H., I'm trans. How did you know?

Which, she realizes as she's saying it, is exactly the worst possible question she could have started with.

James is like, I dunno.

Oh.

He takes a hit from the pipe, holds the smoke. Maria waits.

Nah, he says, I mean, it's not like it's super obvious or anything, I just, like, I was like, I dunno.

So Maria asks if he has any coffee and he says he might, yeah, in the freezer, so she gets up and finds an ancient foil bag of pre-ground coffee all frozen together. She winces: this is not how we do coffee in New York. We have grinders and rituals and French presses and thesauruses to describe smells and tastes and mouth feels. James's frozen coffee reminds her of her mom's house growing up. This coffee is kind of depressing but it will wake her up, stave off a headache.

Here's the deal, James H., Maria says spooning coffee into a dusty old coffee maker. Let's start this conversation off again, on the right foot, and steer it away from normative models of understanding transsexuality.

She's like, let's start with this kid's understanding of himself. Herself. Theirself. Wherever James winds up, you don't get to pick a pronoun for someone even if you want to give them one you think they'll like. She's like, his life is going to be perfect, it's going to rule, but then she realizes something.

Wait, she says. James H., are *you* trans?

He literally snorts.

You mean like am I really a girl? Nah.

No, she says. She starts gearing up to explain that the Really The Gender You Were Assigned At Birth model is cisnormative and poisonous, but stops. They'll get to it. The question at hand is more important to address than that one. Maria has her first inkling that even though she's worked out a cosmology in which a bunch of interconnected puzzle pieces of understanding about oppression and misogyny and transphobia and transphobic faux feminism and all the other things that make up the picture of why everybody always thinks trans women are crazy and stupid— she realizes that even though she's built that up for herself, she might not be able to put all the pieces together for someone else. And it sucks. But she pushes it aside for a minute like no, stay on topic.

No I mean do you ever think you might be trans, not are you a trans guy.

Oh, he says. He makes her wait while he takes another heroic lungful. He holds it, exhales, and says, I dunno.

The way he looks over at her after he says that though— scared, maybe a little bit aggressive, but mostly like, do you believe me—makes his answer clear.

17.

There's a thing Maria is used to doing on the Internet. Since nobody really wants to be a trans woman, i.e. nobody wakes up and goes whoa, maybe my life would be better if I transitioned, alienating most of my friends and my family, I wonder what'll happen at work, I'd love to spend all my money on hormones and surgeries, buying a new wardrobe that I don't even understand right now, probably become unlovable and then ending my short life in a bloody murder. In fact, if there's one thing a lifetime of Stockholm syndrome with hegemony gives you, it's a thorough understanding of cultural tropes about trans women.

It came from the older practice of telling everybody who thought they might be trans that they must be absolutely certain that they were trans before they even considered buying some clothes or starting a testosterone blocker. It's the old narrative, the Johns Hopkins in the seventies narrative: the only people who are really trans are the people who knew explicitly from a young age, are pretty without hormones, and can't survive without transitioning. Trans women on the Internet looked around and were like, well, maybe surviving for the first part of your life in the role of a cis dude is an adaptive strategy. Maybe convincing yourself that you could never transition is a defense mechanism that enabled you to survive high school, family, work—but like most defense mechanisms, it wasn't conscious, and like most defense mechanisms, it became a pattern you weren't aware of, and then, like most defense mechanisms, at some point it stopped making your life easier and started making your life harder.

Plus the world has moved on from the narrative that says being trans is something to be avoided at all costs; it's moved on from the narrative that says the only way to be trans is to be young and tiny and pretty and into men and to transition and then disappear. There's a much better understanding of what it means to be trans now: you just are trans. The fact that your transition might not go smoothly because of the shape of your body or the shape of your family or the shape of your personality or the way that your sexuality has been shaped does not mean that therefore you can just decide not to be trans. You can't will it away. Deciding to will it away is a defense mechanism that is inevitably going to fail and you'll be back where you started: trans. Just older and more entrenched in a life that itself is not much more than a coping mechanism designed to keep you from having to be trans in the real world. If you're trans you're trans and if you're obsessed with whether you might be trans you probably are trans.

For a while they were like, you must be entirely certain. Then they were like, I dunno man, it sounds like you're probably trans, you should explore that. Then, eventually, when Maria and the trans women of the Internet couldn't help but notice that they were 100% accurate in their message board diagnoses, they started just saying, Welp, you are definitely trans. Because even on the off chance that somebody finding a trans community to talk to about these things was not, actually, trans—whatever Actually Trans might even mean—maybe hearing somebody say, like, You are trans, would spur some useful thinking. Like, if you're going to decide on your gender for the rest of your life based on what a couple idiots on the Internet tell you, you probably have problems beyond a false diagnosis of transsexuality. Plus, nobody said you had to commit the rest of your life to anything.

So when James says I dunno, Maria's immediate response is something like: I knew it. I knew it. I am so fucking smart. This is the perfect opportunity to lay it out for him.

She says something like, Whoa, you don't know?

I don't know, he says. I mean, I think about it. But, I mean, look at me, you know? I have a job, a girlfriend. What am I going to do, just start wearing dresses?

He looks down at his hands. There's a pipe in one and a lighter in the other. Without really thinking about he brings the pipe to his lips. His lighter thumb twitches but then he's like, wait, this is dumb, it is a dumb idea to smoke right now, and he reaches over and puts it on the computer desk. It feels pretty mature.

18.

The stupid thing is that obviously James knows that transitioning isn't just, like, you put on a dress and go to work. He knows that's what stupid ridiculous people think. And he was already kicking himself for saying really a girl a minute ago. He knows better than that. But it's weird how hard it is to talk about stuff even though you want to talk about it. His brain just shut off and went all stupid.

Maria really wants to talk about it though .

She's like, So it's something you've thought about?

And he's like, I don't know, I guess so.

And she's like, Like, seriously?

He's like, I don't know, I guess so.

She has this gleam in her eye like she is just so totally stoked that James is telling her this but his brain is freezing up even more, like there are a hundred million things he wants to say but he wants to say them all at once so all he can say is like, Do you wanna smoke? and I dunno and Uhhh, and Duuuhhhh. He sees pizza boxes and dust in the corners of the room, a layer of dust on everything, and he can't quite get his head around the fact that this person is here and in his apartment.

Maria is like, So you knew I was trans?

And James is like, I dunno, yeah.

Because obviously you don't just tell someone you could tell they were trans and how do you tell someone that you figured out they were trans and that the reason you could tell isn't anything they did or anything about them, it's because probably on some level every day you're looking at everyone and hoping you can figure out evidence that they are trans so you can make friends with someone who is trans who can tell you that you are trans too and like solve that problem for you?

Anyway she winces but then she, like, she shakes herself almost, like when a dog is totally flipping out about finding a dead animal that's been run over a bunch of times but it knows it's not going to be allowed to eat the dead animal so it backs away a couple of steps and shakes itself off like it's soaked, like it just climbed out of a river, like it's trying to reset its nervous system or whatever. Or whatever the opposite of that feeling is, the bad version of finding a carcass you're excited to lick, either way she shakes it off and she goes, Yeah.

James goes, Yeah.

She's like, Well, uh, I guess if you want to talk about it I transitioned a long time ago and I know a lot about trans stuff and mostly I came back into the Wal-Mart because I kinda guessed that you were trans but I wasn't sure but you kind of looked, um, exactly like me when I was twenty and I was like, I wish I had had somebody to talk to about this stuff when I was that age, instead of just the stupid 2002 Internet?

James has this weird feeling of dots connecting, or like the fog of being a dumbass stoner from the desert who works at Wal-Mart was lifting for a second, like maybe a moment of clarity or whatever. Because honestly since she asked if he was trans it was like this fog descended, like not weed smoke but something thicker, and he checked out pretty hard. Which made him want to smoke more, even though he was already smoking and smoking. But it was like for a second a beam of light cut through that fog and all these things hit him at once: she's trans but she's not like the weirdo trans people on the Internet. No offense. And: I think I just told someone out loud that I think about being a girl sometimes, even if I didn't admit how much or how bad I think about it. And like, at the same time, there are these two conflicting feelings: like, on one hand, who the fuck is this girl trying to talk to me about shit I don't want to talk about, but on the other hand, maybe I could get into her car and leave town with her and live with her and wear her clothes and bum her hormones and maybe everything would be totally okay forever. So James feels a little bit like his breath got punched out of him but also like this new and better kind of breath got punched into him? Or something, it was weird.

But all he could say was, Yeah, the Internet. It's like sometimes I think about being a girl but I would want to be like Nicole, you know, not like these ladies with the makeup and the boring stupid jokes and beige shoes or whatever the fuck

Yeah, Maria says, The problem with the Internet is that most of the trans women who manage to transition and still be dirtbags or punkers or weirdos or dykes or radicals or whatever stay way away from those people, too, and there's this narrative of 'deep stealth' that makes it seem like maybe we don't exist or we stop being trans but actually what happens is that we keep living our lives and being dirty weirdos we just—I should only speak for myself, I guess, but I just got bored of talking about it. Like, I have a livejournal, and I know some people on the Facebook who

I've met IRL a couple times but mostly, like, the Advocate doesn't want anything to do with trans women who can't afford face surgeries and hate capitalism so it can even just be hard to meet anyone

James is like, Well I don't know anything about capitalism or anything.

Maria is like, Well let's talk.

James is like, We are talking.

Maria laughs and James is like, What.

Okay sorry, Maria says, Let's not talk about capitalism or anarchism or anything except I do want to say that those things ended up being totally essential to my understanding of being trans and feminism and my location and the things that suck about being trans. All that stuff. So maybe like we can table them for now and get back to them.

James is like, Okay.

Maria's like, Well, what do you want to talk about?

James thinks for a second, and then thinks for another second, and then when he realizes that actually he's probably too stoned to come up with anything he's like, Do you want breakfast?

She gives him a look like I can see that this dumb kid's brain is full and says, Yeah, sure, probably.

19

The only food James has is some old peanut butter, some bread in the freezer, and the butt end of that bag of shitty coffee, so they eat peanut butter toast and make more weak coffee. Having Maria in his kitchen makes James feel like his kitchen is a dusty, grungy and kind of sad mess, in a way that having Nicole in there never really does. He's like, I guess my apartment sucks. Weird how you don't notice that.

So they make food and he still kind of feels like his head is in orbit or whatever but eating food and changing the subject makes him feel like maybe intense stuff is put away even though probably in his body and his nerves he's still feeling it. Like he is probably kind of lightheaded.

They don't talk for a while, they just kind of make food and eat it or whatever but then out of nowhere Maria is like, You've been to Reno, right?

James is like, Yeah.

She's like, You wanna go to Reno? Right now?

I don't know, he says, mouth all stuck together with peanut butter, I kind of have to go to work this afternoon or whatever.

Your call, Maria says, But you kind of have to ask yourself, do I want to have the kind of life where I call out of work to go to Reno with a cool wingnut stranger lady, or do I want to have the kind of life where I work loyally for Wal-Mart until I die?

There is probably some middle ground between the two and also that kind of felt like a weird and manipulative thing to say, but thinking about it and swallowing James is kind of like, well, I guess I actually do want to have the kind of life where I bail on work to go to Reno with a transgender murderess I just met or whatever. And the more he thinks about it the more he's like, whoa, this is actually what freedom feels like. Deciding to skip work to hang out with a stranger feels like something people in Star City don't do, but it is probably something that cool people with weird hair and clothes he wouldn't even know how to put on, like in Portland or Austin or something, probably do.

Okay, he says, But like what are we going to even do in Reno? Gamble?

Dude we are going to party as hell, she says.

Oh.

Yeah dude.

You know I'm not old enough to drink though right?

She makes a face like hmm and then swallows.

Well uh, she says. Then she's like, Nah, never mind.

He's like, What, and she's like, Uh, well, this is kind of a weird offer but I kind of have a bunch of heroin?

20

At this point James has to acknowledge this feeling that's been creeping up and down his spine since he first saw her at Wal-Mart but which so far he's been able to ignore. He's like: who the fuck is this person in my apartment.

Probably she can see that he's kind of weirded out so she starts talking but he kind of talks over her, he's like, Uhhhhh, who are you? Like for real, all I know about you is that you're trans and you have a pretend dog and cat and maybe you have pretend heroin, too, but maybe it's real? What are you doing here?

She's just like, Yeah, okay, and then neither of them knows what to say so again James is like, For real, who are you.

Maria is sitting on the floor and James is on the futon. She looks up at him from across the room with her bangs in her eyes, pushes her hair back off her forehead—her kind of big forehead—and sighs.

Okay, she says. Sure. I'm twenty-nine. I grew up in a shitty little cow town in Pennsylvania, moved to New York City after college, transitioned six years ago, and work in a bookstore. Well. I guess I used to work in a bookstore. I don't know. Like a month ago I figured out that I was really unhappy with my life so I borrowed-stole my girlfriend's car and, like, I guess I just pointed it west.

James thinks, like, yeah and you're a heroin addict? And like, you were inevitably unhappy with your life because you're trans, right? Meaning, transition doesn't work. But what he says is, It took you a month to drive a couple thousand miles?

She smirks at him and pushes her hair back again. I dunno, she says. I guess so. I did a lot of hanging out in parking lots and stuff.

James goes, Like, on heroin?

She laughs kind of too loud.

Nah, she says, That whole thing is fuckin stupid. When I was like sixteen, I had a friend who was really into heroin, right? Used to buy hundreds of dollars worth at a time, right, and just do it recreationally. Shootin heroin on a Friday night. Or a Tuesday night, didn't matter. It was, like, dumb teenage shit. Check out how tough we are. I latched onto him. When he'd go to Philadelphia and buy four hundred dollars worth, I'd give him a twenty and have him bring me back a couple dimebags. Whatever. No big deal.

She stops talking for a second and then nods, like she's figuring out how much of this story to tell him, and she's decided: all of it.

So yeah check this out, she says. I sort of just broke up with my girlfriend. We had been together for a bunch of years and developed this routine where we had an apartment and cats and stuff and our bills were under control, she had a grownup job that was turning her into a grownup kind of, and I realized. Like. I guess I just figured out that I wasn't happy, right? I was blaming her for stuff and getting pissed that she was turning into a grownup or whatever but mostly I was just so checked out that I didn't even understand if I was mad or sad or confused or what, you know?

James is like, I *do* know.

So some dumb stuff happened, Maria says, and then we broke up and I was like, well shit, the problem is that I've been trying to be responsible, and accountable to everyone else, and to make sure that nobody was freaked out by me or my feelings or desires or whatever. I was like, the solution is to become as irresponsible as I can. Obviously, that turned out to be a totally stupid theory though. Here's the thing James H.: while I was driving across the country, right, and hanging out in like small town parks and route 80 off-ramps and drinking truckstop coffee refills in the middle of the night—what I realized was, that was not a pattern that started in my relationship with Steph. This was a pattern that went back my whole fucking life. I was totally checked out in high school, to the point that it seemed like a good idea to try a little heroin now and then. I barely made facial expressions in grade school. I learned to fake it well enough that people didn't mistake me for an autistic kid; actually, it's fucking wild if you think about it, how well being totally checked out emotionally can look like normal American masculinity. So looking back I was like, holy shit, I don't remember much about being a little kid, but I must've checked out of my life: meaning, like, started the pattern that me and Steph broke up over. When I was a little kid, when I started to develop a personality and a gender and to express that personality and gender, a tiny little dirtbag punker who didn't know anything about being trans or saying I want to be a girl. Or: I am a girl. Who only knew that she wanted to be in Poison, to dress and act like the rock stars who were boys but who got to wear all the makeup and outfits. Everybody everywhere started socializing that stuff out of me. I was an observant kid, you know, I looked around and I was like, well shit, I'd better listen to these messages I'm getting from TV and from the grownups around me, instead of whatever the fuck my obviously incorrect brain is telling me. You know? Being completely checked out, that shit started when I was a tiny little kid.

I started really hating myself when I figured this out, like, in a way that I'd never even felt before. Like my fuckin' astral hate chakra had been revitalized. I was like, whoa, I have a lifetime's worth of unprocessed shut-down emotions to work through, so it's a good thing I'm by myself out here. I thought about it and wrote about it and stuff and eventually, when I was like, cool, I have all this heroin, it'd probably be easier to overdose and die than it would be to work through, what, twenty-five years of self-invalidating habit? So I called my friend Piranha, who's always been way leveler-headed than me, and she was like, Hey stupid, did you ever stop to think that that pattern, that coping mechanism, was actually a brilliant strategy to keep yourself alive? She was like, listen up dummy, when you are a little kid and it is the mid-eighties, saying 'I need to be a girl' is not the sort of thing that tends to be met with love and appreciation. It is the sort of thing that tends to get met with, Well you are a boy and We'd better butch him up and Welp we had ourselves a little freak baby, that sucks, and Shut the fuck up, junior. Piranha was like, Maria you dolt, the smartest thing you could have done in that no-win situation was to be like, Okay, I'll play your game until I'm old enough to run away from it and figure out my own stupid game. She was like, Which you did, right? You moved to New York. You transitioned. You fuckin solved it. The problem wasn't the coping mechanism, the problem is that the coping mechanism become a pattern of behavior, and it is really hard to just up and end a behavior pattern.

I was like, Piranha, man, why the fuck aren't you fuckin rich, you are a genius, I said this kind of through tears, and she was like, Uh, Maria, I'm not rich because I'm trans and because I'm a woman. I was like, Oh yeah.

So anyway I spent the last couple weeks thinking about that stuff, right, thinking about how to reset those patterns, and how to, like, have feelings? And I was like, fuck, uh, re-reading a bunch of Pema Chodron and Thich Nhat Hanh would probably be a really productive thing to do right now; snorting a mountain of heroin would probably be, like, the opposite. Which made me think about the role of drugs and alcohol and stuff in my life and made me want to go straightedge and then once you're straightedge you might as well go vegan and then I was like, actually, I'm coasting on my almost no savings, I can't really afford to go vegan right now. You know? So I'm stuck with all this heroin, and I'm not going to try to fucking become a heroin dealer.

So basically, I'm like, who the fuck are you, Maria Griffiths? A fucking idiot, is who.

21.

James just listens while Maria goes off and finds himself
kind of trusting her. Like not that much, obviously she has
her shit and stuff, but if you're going to have a story about
why you're claiming to have a bunch of heroin, that's a
pretty good one. And he starts to think, Well, maybe it
would be worth it to take a trip to Reno with this person.

He knows he probably didn't understand, like, two thirds
of what she's said. Hello: he is a checked-out fucking stoner,
right, his life isn't exactly hers but he's been the weird kid
his whole life, right, and he's been jealous of girls his whole
life, right, so like, maybe that means something? But at the
same time he's like, god, this girl is a fucking mess, and
the more you look, the more you can kind of tell that she's
trans just by looking at her. And he keeps thinking about
that flash of forehead. Whatever.

What happens if you sprinkle heroin on a bowl of weed?

His brain is all full but he hears himself say, Yeah, I could
go to Reno with you.

She's like, That's your response to that? To everything I
just told you?

He's like, I dunno.

She laughs. All right, she says, Yeah word, let's go to Reno. But James H., I want you to tell me who you are, too. Your turn. Charon's fare.

Maria disappears into the bathroom for five minutes. Then they finish the shitty coffee and bail.

22.

The first thing they do in the car is to drive through a coffee place so Maria can get real coffee. It's a little drive-through coffee hut by the highway and she gets kind of mad when there are no bagels. When James doesn't get any coffee she's like, Oh, do you want some downers instead, reaches over to pop open the glove box, and gestures at a blue-striped athletic sock rolled up in another sock and tucked under some maps and a literal pair of raggedy gloves with the fingertips cut off. He's like, really, that's where you keep your heroin, just in a sock in the glovebox? Then they're on route 80 and he's kind of like, still mostly wrapping his head around the stuff Maria told him back in the apartment, trying to figure out how to talk about himself in a similar way.

I mean, he thinks, what the fuck *is* my deal? I am a dumbass stoner who's fucking shitty at being in relationships, too, only I'm not breaking up with my girlfriend. But also this overwhelmed feeling is dissolving into a feeling of, like, coming down and feeling kind of excited. He hasn't smoked since before they ate breakfast.

So, Maria says when they've been on the highway for a minute, What's your deal, James H.?

Ha, he says, Okay. I just turned twenty, I grew up in Star City Nevada, which is a stupid fucking town and I hate it, and I've worked at Wal-Mart since I was sixteen. I have a girlfriend named Nicole. She's cool but we're kind of in a fight, I should text her. My parents live here too, I see my mom kind of a lot. I don't know.

She does this, like, studied and intentional staring straight forward kind of thing, where it's like he can tell that she wants him to talk about gender stuff or whatever but he has no idea what to say. Every time it seems like he comes up with something concrete to mention—like, masturbation, or sex, or fantasies, or finding himself crying in the boys' bathroom line at camp when he was eight—it seems like there are eight or twelve things to say about it and all of them are important and since he can't pick one he doesn't say any of them. Sex with Nicole? The dress in his closet? Stupid Internet porn? Is now the time to explore whether smoking hella weed is a cover story for whatever the fuck it's a cover story for? Fuck all that. And like... how much does this relate to the stuff Nicole always says about how she wishes he would just make a decision? It's all too connected to even start to pick apart to talk about. He draws a line in the dust on the dashboard, right next to the air vent, exhales, sees that his skinny pale fingers are shaking, and breathes in.

But James is like, no way, that breath he just took was for saying something real and stupid left-wing radio can't take that away from him. Instead of letting that breath go, he talks, loud, over the radio.

He's like, Do you know what autogynephilia is?

Maria does like a cross between an exhalation and an Ooooooh. Like, oh, that is a shame. But what she says is, Yes, I know about that.

Okay, he says. Well, sometimes I think I like, have autogynephilia? Or am an autogynephiliac, if that's a thing.

There's this long, tense silence and James wants to get his weed out of his messenger bag and just smoke right up, right now, but you can't just change the subject like that. The silence goes on for a really long time but probably not, like, that long, and then Maria laughs. Like, pretty hard. James is like, are you fucking kidding me, but he doesn't say it out loud.

Maria's like, Yeah I know about that. I um. What do you mean, when you say you are an autogynephile?

I don't know, he says, feeling immediately cornered and angry, which might be kind of weird. Like she did just correct him, kind of subtly, but who cares, it's more than that. This shit isn't really funny though and it's ruining his life, so he's like, I don't know, I'm like, into girls and stuff, but I guess like, mostly what I'm... turned on by... is being a girl? Like, not just being a girl but like. You know. I don't know, it's complicated.

He realizes he's angry and glaring out the window, lighting cactuses on fire with the rage in his squinty-eyed fury or whatever.

Maria is like, Can I tell you about autogynephilia, James H.?

23

Sure, he mutters, not even really sure why he suddenly feels so fucked up.

Check this out, she says. When I was younger, right, it was really easy to just not be invested in myself or what was going on. I could wear shapeless clothes, have relationships with people where we just talked about bands and video games and, y'know, nothing, and never went deeper than that. It was all super easy, right? This is that checked-out pattern I was talking about before. When people think you're a dude, they pretty much expect that shit from you. But the only time I couldn't lie to myself about who I wanted to be, and how I wanted to be, and like, the way I needed to exist in the world if I was going to actually exist in the world, is when I was jacking off.

James's squinty-eyed glare pops open pretty wide at the fact that this girl he met yesterday was talking about jacking off with him, but he doesn't say anything.

I was thinking about being a girl while I jacked off, she says, Like, as soon as I started jacking off. For years I thought it was because I was a pervert, that I had this kink I must never, ever tell anyone about, right? Which was sad.

There weren't really any misogynist or otherwise fucked up connotations to the specifics of what I was thinking about—I just wanted to be a woman, which gets framed as *a priori* quote unquote '*perverted*.' Right? Like the only unperverted kind of sex is being a dude and getting a boner from looking at a girl's boobs and then putting the boner in her vagina. But guess what, that shit is all culturally constructed and culturally bound, blah blah blah. My point is just, like, then I got online, and I started looking at porn made by people who had the same alleged kink as me and I was like, why is this all so fucking stupid and misogynist and poorly written and just, like, disgusting—but since there wasn't really much gender-change erotica or whatever that wasn't totally fucked up, I ended up spending a ton of time with some totally creepy and busted stuff. It took years for me to come to understand that the things that are hot in that shitty porn—the power exchange, the specific gestures and accoutrements and paradigms—can exist separate from the totally fucked up way they get implemented by the people making that porn.

Which guess what, she says, There is a good reason for that: cool dykes, and I guess probably dudes and probably straight girls too, I don't know, whatever, they've published a lot of work about being a responsible pervert! But pretty much everybody making porn with trans women in it is a man. Like, someone who is invested in his own male privilege, and in reifying power systems where he is on top, and in deeply misogynistic constructions of what it means to be a woman and therefore what it means and looks like to quote unquote 'become' a woman, and just like, all this stuff. It's complicated and gross but the point of it is just, that porn is produced by a misogynist paradigm by people who don't even give a fuck about questioning misogyny. In a way they're eroticizing misogyny, which, like, is totally cool if you're doing it intentionally and consciously, but when you're doing it and oops you are reinforcing it as a cultural norm, fuck you. Like, seriously, fuck you.

Put that aside for a second, she says. The term autogynephilia was made up by a psychologist. It was popularized by this guy J Michael Bailey, who mostly studies deviant sexuality.

I know about J Michael Bailey, James says.

Okay, she said. So he writes this book explaining that there are two kinds of transsexual women. There's homosexual transsexuals, who were gay men before transitioning and who become attractive to heterosexual men after transitioning, and then autogynephilic transsexuals, who just have such a big hot boner for being women that they decide to become women even though they are ugly and unlovable.

I know about this, James says, still kind of pissed, partly because he doesn't know how to talk about his own shit and partly because Maria was explaining a bunch of stuff that he already knew about.

Okay but humor me, she says. Ignoring for a second the weird asymmetry here—if you are trans then you are either hot for men or for yourself. And ignoring for a second the total lack of feminist analysis, 'homosexual transsexuals' make pretty women not because they are already familiar and comfortable with being the object of the male gaze, but instead because they are into men. And ignoring—obviously—the glaring fact that queer theorists, and generations of feminists before them, have shown clearly that sex and gender are separate from each other, and that sexuality is related to, but not produced by them. Ignoring all these things, let's ask the obvious question: what is the parallel paradigm in women? Where are the autoandrophiles?

Actually, they're around, she says, But the point isn't that these are somehow legitimate labels that get misapplied. It's the whole framework, how inherently by making the conversation about the classification of trans women into a conversation about trans women's sexuality, you've already determined that the defining characteristic of trans women is their sexuality. The alleged 'science' of autogynephilia is about making up categories to understand why J Michael Bailey wants to bone some trans women but not others. It's about framing trans women as men in order to understand deviant male sexuality, without ever looking at female sexuality. Has anybody ever done a study where they used cis women as a control group to compare trans women to? I don't fucking know. Further: do trans women who are attracted to women who aren't themselves even exist?

It's all totally fucking stupid, she finishes.

She sounds kind of choked up or whatever so James looks over and she actually is about to start crying.

So he's like, Uh, okay. Because he doesn't really understand what she had just said.

It's just that once you start using their terms, she says, You're putting yourself into this restrictive box they made up that doesn't leave room for figuring out who you are or what you want. It's a box labeled Dude and Pervert—Bad and Terrible Secret. When in my experience it shouldn't have to be a secret that if you're a woman, you might be hot for being a woman when it's an appropriate time to be hot; when, in fact, if you are a woman—trans or cis—it makes sense to like the idea of being a woman in bed. It's not a perversion at all. It's like the opposite of being a pervert. It's the least perverted thing, for your sexuality to match your gender! So like, autogynephilia theory just is basically designed to reinforce the idea that trans women are men, and that women don't have sexualities, and that straight dudes are good people to talk about queer women's sexualities.

Okay but I didn't even say I was transgender, James says. I don't know what I am, but I do know that autogynephilia kind of fits so whatever.

Well yeah but even still, she says, pausing for a second, Our kinks aren't just random things that happened to us. They tell us things: wanting to get tied up is usually about the deep, fucked up and normative coercive relationships we have to the different kinds of freedom; wanting to have somebody spank you is usually in some way about shame. In practice these are really complicated things and they're complicated by any number of other factors but let's be real here about the fact that when we're not allowed to have something we want, we get all fuckin' weird about it. Sometimes that weirdness looks like a kink. That kink is even stronger when it's you that's doing the denying. What's the relationship between fetish and taboo, you know? Whether or not you're trans. Being hot for being a girl makes sense if you're a girl who's not allowed to be a girl. It is like the opposite of complicated.

James hears a hitch or a pause in her voice at the end there that makes it clear that she thinks he's a dumb kid who just doesn't understand yet that he's transsexual so he just keeps glaring and doesn't say anything and she drops it. They're quiet for a bit and then she puts on a CD with a dude yelling kind of high pitched and guitars that sounded like they were scraping the metal walls of a rusty shed. It's awful. James wishes that he'd rolled a joint ahead of time so he could smoke it right now, because you can't really roll down the highway blazing a pipe. But he hadn't had the foresight.

He thinks Maria has not only decided that he needs to transition, probably pretty soon, and that he should break up with Nicole and stop smoking weed and probably, like, wear a ton of clothes all at the same time and dye his hair red and talk in long, boring monologues. He's kind of like, Well fuck you then. But he still can't bring himself to just be like, Fuck you, and never talk to her again. He imagines having the kind of fight you have when you're friends, where you make up afterward, but he's only known her for a day and has no idea how to argue like that. He's probably never had that kind of fight with anyone. So he sits and sulks and glares at the cactuses.

Getting Stoned And Glaring At Cactuses: The James Hanson Story. Written and directed by Charlie Kaufman.

Hold on, he says. I gotta pee.

Okay cool me too, she says.

24.

The thing about route 80 is that there's nothing on it—
like, there are truck stops at every exit, and there are exits
every ten miles or so, but James didn't even really have to
take a piss. Like, kind of he did but really what he wanted
to do was get high. Like he felt the need to get high. Right
now. He should've smoked before they left the house but
at the time he'd been like man, this is some intense shit
right here, I better be sober for it, but now shit has gotten
even more intense and he's kind of feeling done with it.
Ready to be high. It's been a weird twenty-four hours.
Whatever. Anyway most of the exits off 80 in the area have
those big Flying J truck stops or whatever and you can't
really smoke weed in their huge bathrooms but there's a
dusty old piece of shit gas station at the Lovelock exit with
a men's room and a women's room that only fit one person
at a time and the doors lock. So that shit was a brilliant
tactic: Oh, hey, I have to pee, let's pull off at the next exit.
Turns out James is a brilliant strategist. Who knew.

Probably everybody knew that he was a genius when it
came to weed, actually.

They pull into the gas station and it's as desolate as ever. Maria parks at the pump and puts gas in her tank before she goes to pee, which makes him wonder if she's secretly rich or what, but who cares. Then he gets distracted thinking about how if you wanted to make a big boring metaphor about who goes into which bathroom at this stupid gas station you could, but he doesn't even want to think about it so he locks himself into the men's room, packs a bowl, and blazes up. Whatever.

He smokes the whole thing and packs another but while he's packing the second bowl he has this conscientious feeling and only packs it halfway full. Like, hey man, you don't have to smoke two whole bowls. A bowl and a half should be enough to get whatever feelings you're having under control.

He imagines the smoke billowing out of the bathroom behind him, like he always does, but leaving the bathroom is not dramatic. It feels good to be stoned though. The sun is above them and hot even though it's November. There's nothing around but desert and a bleached-out little gas station store with probably candy bars and stuff in it. He has this long-distance bleak feeling, like it's the end of the world and they came out here. It's a dumb Resident Evil movie or maybe even an old western. James always kind of felt insecure about the fact that he couldn't bring himself to give a fuck about westerns, given that he is a westerner, but he can take 'em or leave 'em, no strong feelings either way. He doesn't even actually care about country music, you just can't help but absorb it through your skin when you live in Star City. He sure doesn't have any Brad Paisley mp3s or anything. He's staring at the fancy-looking wheel of the front tire of the fancy bike chained to the back of Maria's car when she walks up to him, out of nowhere, makes eye contact, and starts laughing.

Oh yeah, she says. Meaning, Oh yeah, you're a stoner waste of space who can't do anything without getting high.

She probably didn't mean like, that specifically.

But James can hear it in her voice so he mumbles something and they get back into the car. The same CD is playing but obviously it is a lot more interesting now and he can sit and listen to it and space out. Eventually, when they're back on the highway and he hasn't said anything for a while, Maria starts singing along quietly a little bit sometimes, under her breath. She has kind of a low singing voice but he can't hear it well enough to say more than that about it. He can't tell if she sounds like a guy or a girl or what, she just sounds quiet.

Mostly though he's focusing on himself and on why he kind of hates her and himself and everything right now, because like, he is supposed to be on this cool adventure right now, but all he can think about is this really shitty stuff. The things about this girl that seem gross, that stubble that's gone now, her stupid forehead, the things about himself that he hates, the things about his relationship with Nicole that are good and that he should be thankful for. He should probably text her, but the thing about texting when he's high is that he never really got good at it. It's like how on the Internet you look like a fucking dork if you use emoticons, but nobody knows what you're talking about if you're sarcastic or anything. He's good at being a stoner—let's be real, maybe the best—but he can never figure out how a sentence in a text message is going to be read, like whether it'll seem sarcastic or mean or whatever. Like, Maria probably thinks he should send a text like, I think we need to spend some time apart, but that makes him feel even more like he should send a text that says I think we should never spend any time apart. Even though, like, two nights ago he was thinking, I think we should spend some time apart.

And to be real, this is day two apart.

He looks down and his body is all scrunched up, knees to his chest in the little passenger seat of this little car. He's pretty tall, which is important for a lot of reasons, but he's making himself tiny.

Whatever, he stretches out his legs, moves the seat as far back as it'll go and rubs his shoulder. His shoulders are sore. Who cares about anything. He doesn't need to solve this right now. The singer is yowling about how merchandise keeps us in line and James is thinking, like, this is not relevant to my life right now, but he doesn't want to think about himself and his shit any more so he doesn't say anything.

After a while Maria asks James if he told his girlfriend he was going to Reno.

He hadn't even thought about telling her. That's weird right? Usually he would check in with her right away about whatever he does but right now he hadn't really thought much past, like, I guess I will go to Reno with this person who I thought I liked. Maybe on some level he figured he'd be back before Nicole got off work today. Either way he's like, No, and Maria asks what Nicole is like.

She's cool, James says. I dunno.

That's it?

What's your girlfriend like? he shoots back.

Okay yeah fair question, she says. Except we broke up. She's cool though. She's kind of like, y'know how sometimes you know a punker when he's fourteen and then you meet him ten years later and you're like, man, you are an entirely different person, it's like you never even had a punk phase, with your cell phone and your button-down shirt and your haircut? But sometimes you meet a punker you knew when he was fourteen ten years later and you're like, whoa, your punkerness has grown and matured and evolved into a worldview that's obviously consistent with what you believed when you were younger?

James thinks, No, but he doesn't say anything.

Steph is definitely the latter, Maria says, except like, instead of punk, really it's like her babydyke purple hair and triangle pins evolved into this, not power lesbian, exactly, but this grownup queer thing.

She thinks for a minute.

I guess it's kind of scary, she says. I guess watching your girlfriend become someone else, more of a grownup, but still stay herself, while meanwhile you're still working the same job you always have, at the same level of broke with the same people who knew you years ago and knew you when you transitioned. When you see the same people every day that you've seen since before you transitioned and you already went through this massive social and physical change, and you're afraid to really even consider changing or evolving in any way, because you kind of had to have all this bravado, to act like you really believed in yourself in order to transition.

It's like, how do you take down that bravado in order to evolve as a person? I mean, you asked about Steph and I'm just talking about myself again but I guess the question is, like, how do you transition but then continue to evolve as a person, post-transition, when it seems like the only way you got through your transition was to assert loudly, even just to yourself, that you knew who you were and you knew what you wanted and you trusted yourself?

I think Steph has been in the process of figuring out who she is and what she needs and I've been in the non-process of, like, swearing up and down forever that I knew exactly who I was and exactly what I needed and what I cared about. I think, James H., that I was swearing to myself before I left New York that the most important thing in my life was irresponsibility but what I meant, what I hadn't figured out yet, was that I don't need to be irresponsible in every way. I think what I meant was that I need to stop feeling responsible, to everybody all the time, for presenting this consistent and static face. And I needed to get over the idea that being responsible in a relationship means being consistent and stoic and out of touch with my own feelings.

What a bunch of dude bullshit to have internalized.

But yeah, she says, Steph rules and is smart and good at what she's doing—she's definitely the kid who kept her principles. She works at fucking Callen-Lorde when she's not at work! I guess she's kind of a fucking idiot, still, pulling weird plots about pretending to cheat on me or whatever, but I think I couldn't keep up with her because I didn't know how to be in a relationship so I just grabbed onto our relationship as tightly as I could and hoped for the best but inevitably I just squeezed all the blood out of it or whatever. Fuck.

So why'd you break up, James asks.

Fuuuuuck, Maria says. I. I don't know.

Oh you don't know, James says, suddenly able to take the offensive.

I mean, Maria says. She makes a face and gestures like she's got all these thoughts and ideas and she's going to get them in order and it seems like she's just gathering her thoughts but then it takes a really long time and eventually she's like, I don't know.

Oh you just don't know? James says. Like nobody cheated on anybody and you didn't just stop having interests in common and you still liked all the same movies and you just looked up one day and you were like, Well see you, I think I'm gonna steal your fucking car and drive it thousands of miles to fucking Star City Nevada for no fucking reason?

Maria pauses for a second and then she's like, It's complicated.

No fuckin shit, James says, glad he's kind of stoned because sober he certainly couldn't twist the knife like this. You just complicatedly stole her car and bailed.

I don't know, all right? Maria says. I just fuckin'—Some shit happened and then it wasn't like we suddenly hated each other or anything. I was just like, fuck, this relationship isn't good for me any more and she was like Yeah me neither and I was like Well. And she was like, Well, cool. And then instead of working out the logistics of the most important breakup in my three decades of life I fuckin just bailed, okay? Yeah. I'm gonna have to go to New York at some point and get my books and my cat and shit but no, I don't have a tidy narrative about how we broke up.

So you broke up with her, James says.

She pauses even longer and then she's like, It was a mutual thing.

James stares at the cactuses muttering about how Yeah fuckin' right, it was a fuckin mutual thing. I've dated exactly one fuckin' girl in my life and I know that 'It was a mutual thing' means I got my ass dumped so fuckin' hard. Fuckin' delusional ass—but he stops himself before he says dyke.

He laughs. He's not sure whether he said any of this loud enough to hear, but then Maria laughs—once, a little—and she's like, She broke up with me.

James is like, Whatever.

Maria's like, So. Does Nicole know about the old autogynephilia?

James has a cold panic reaction, like, God I hope not, and then he goes, Not as far as I know.

Why not?

Can you imagine if you had a boyfriend who told you that shit?

He thinks for a second. Then he's like, Wait a minute, you know exactly why the fuck not, I thought you knew all this shit and that was why you were stepping in and trying to get me to break up with Nicole and be transgender or whatever the fuck.

Maria doesn't say anything so he's like Fuck man, I don't know, how the fuck do you tell your girlfriend something like that?

He's thinking, though, that the reason he's unhappy with Nicole is the exact same reason Maria was saying she was unhappy with Steph. He's like, it's not because I am transgender, it's not because I'm a fucking pervert, it's because I don't say, like, I think this movie sucks. Or, I don't want to eat that. Or, I want to wear your underwear, I want to have a pussy like yours.

It feels like one leads to the other. Like if he were to say, I don't want to watch a stupid Drew Carey movie, Nicole would be like Okay, what do you want to watch and he'd be honest and be like Paris Is Burning, or Hedwig and the Angry Inch, or Transamerica, some other movie about transgender people that he can barely even admit to himself that he wants to watch. And then if he was honest about what movie he wanted to watch when Nicole comes over the whole castle would tumble down and it would lead to being honest about what kind of clothes he wants, and what kind of body he'd want to have so he could look okay in those clothes, and then questions about what kind of sex he wants to have—which he doesn't even know how to answer—and that was when it just, like, sank in. That all the shit Maria had been talking about, the whole time, was exactly all of his own shit. Like different specifics. Kind of. But like, what *are* my kinks telling me? Why am I so unable to talk to Nicole? She asks, clearly, all the time, what I'm thinking and what I want, but I don't even know how to tell her, even if the answers were things that she'd want to hear.

But what he says is, kind of spiteful, Whatever, Maria. What are your kinks? What are they telling *you* about yourself?

25.

She doesn't say anything. For like, forty minutes or something.

26.

They're getting close and then he spaces out, and Maria sees it first. She's like, Check it out. The green highway sign says, Reno, and there's an arrow.

They pull off the highway and she's like, Look, and then she's like, What are we even doing? I mostly wanted to hang out with you because you look exactly like me when I was twenty and I thought maybe you had some gender stuff so I was like, Well, maybe this is a chance for me to do some good in the world and give you a space to talk about it. But I'm obviously doing a shitty job. So let's start over okay? Shit got fucking intense and you're right. I'm just monologuing so let's talk about something else, something totally unrelated.

Okay, yeah, James says. Sure, cool. Let's reboot. What do you want to talk about?

Haha, she says. I don't know, man, what do you want to talk about?

I don't know. Movies?

Sure! she says, banging the steering wheel with her hand. Did you see the movie with the monster in New York City and the first half you're like, I just wish a monster would just kill these fucking yuppies, and then the monster spends the whole rest of the movie, like, picking them off one by one? I think it's still in the theater.

James is like, No.

27

He can't think of a movie to talk about. He hates all the ones he's seen in the last year or two and the ones he likes suddenly seem deeply stupid. Neither of them says anything and then before they're even in Reno proper Maria pulls off the road into the parking lot of a little burrito restaurant and goes, We need to eat something. I'm being weird because I'm hungry. Are you?

I guess so, James says. He hadn't thought about it.

She gets out of the car before she can really answer, though, and like bounces straight into the restaurant. He can see her through this window that runs the whole width of the restaurant, looking up at the menu above the register counter, like a McDonald's layout except maybe a little greasier, accumulated grease blackening the corners of the menu board and the little plastic letters that fit into horizontal slots that run the length of the menu. Blackening the space under the registers, in the corners of the tables or whatever. You can't actually see it but that's the impression you get from looking through the window.

He takes a minute and tries to get his head together but when he looks up Maria is standing at the counter of the restaurant, looking back at him, holding up a twenty-dollar bill and pointing at it. Like signalling, Get the fuck in here. I'm buying you lunch, stupid.

As soon as he gets inside what he's thinking about is, like, I wonder if these people working here can tell that Maria is trans. And like, if they can, what do they think of me? Like it almost felt like, they must know she's trans, and then they must know that I'm, like, whatever the fuck I am. Sort of a kind of trans or whatever. Like it wasn't just, they might figure out that I'm into the kind of embarrassing porn that I'm into. It was like, they might figure out something way more embarrassing and fucked up about like what a fucked up fake human being I am, or something. Who knows. But he can't even focus on the menu above the counter. He's like, I know these words, but am I even hungry?

Maria is already at a table and when he looks over she's like, Get whatever.

I don't even know what to get, what should I get?

And she's like, Fuckin' nachos, obviously.

So he orders nachos. She has a Corona and he's like, Holy shit do I want a beer too? but he's only old enough to join the army and die for his country, he's not old enough to drink. He's glad he's still pretty high, though, and glad that at least he's old enough to gamble. There's a video poker TV thing at the table where Maria's sitting and he puts a quarter into it. He loses immediately.

They start to have this sad little lunch in Reno without speaking but after a couple minutes Maria starts talking.

All right, she says. She exhales for a second and then she starts over. Okay. This is kind of about trans stuff but mostly it's about me being a fucking asshole, is that okay?

James actually, legitimately laughs for real, even though Maria is talking about being trans out loud and even though he doesn't recognize anybody right now and it's a pretty long shot, somebody he went to high school with could walk in at any moment, overhear Maria even though she's not talking very loud, figure out that he is an autogynephile. But weirdly he's kind of like, whatever.

He's like yeah, totally.

Here's the thing, Maria says. Nobody pays attention to J. Michael Bailey any more. He's just some dude who wrote a book about how trans women are perverts, which is an easy thing to get a press to publish. You'll never go broke selling regressive 'common sense.' But his buddy Kenneth Zucker is still a big deal. He runs this clinic in Canada and advocates like—

She makes a face and stops, aware that she's already started monologuing.

Look, you know NPR, she asks.

Kind of, he says.

There was a show on NPR a couple weeks ago where they had this woman. A doctor, who was like, Well listen, if your kid is trans, you should be nice to them and support them. Kids are smart. And then there was this other doctor, Ken Zucker, who was like, Well no, actually, if your kid is trans, what you have to do is be really mean to them. Get them to cry all the time. We have no evidence that this works, but do you want your kid to be a sick fucking weirdo pervert when they grow up? Fucking your kid up so your kid represses everything and forgets how to feel anything for decades, until she realizes she has hated her whole life and needs to transition, that is what we recommend up here in Canada.

And they were both in the studio, Maria says, And you could call in.

So I called in, right, fully expecting to lay it out for him—even though this other doctor, doctor Ehrensomething, was already doing a good job laying it out. But I was going to call in and be like Hey, I'm trans, and do you really want to say that shit to my face? Do you really want to tell me that I'd be better off if my childhood had been even harder? Even though I know, from personal experience, that people won't listen to you about trans stuff just because you're trans. Nobody cares about the 'well, from personal experience I can tell you' that precedes the 'what you think you know is wrong.' But I was still like, what am I going to do, not call in? So I get through and the dude, the radio host, introduces me. He goes, We have a caller on the line, Dr. Zucker, who says she's a trans woman from Pennsylvania and she strongly disagrees with your perspective. Maria?

And I'm like, Yeah! Here it is! I'm gonna solve this shit once and for all! Except I open my mouth and nothing comes out, right. I had thought, maybe I'll get all carried away and flip out on this asshole! And I'd thought, maybe I'll just rationally lay out the contradiction inherent in this guy's argument, right. But I hadn't thought of a first sentence to even start out with. If I had been like, Hello Dr. Zucker, I probably could have started. But instead I froze up in the face of institutionalized patriarchal misogyny, ageism and transphobia and I couldn't say anything. There was this long pause and then Terry Gross was like, Maria, are you there? But I still couldn't say anything and I guess they cut off my call but not before you hear me let out half of this one pathetic, desperate sob. You can listen to it online, I checked.

She stops and James kind of wishes she'd go on.

Fuck, he says.

Yeah, she says.

He puts another quarter into the video poker machine and he's like, So you didn't get to talk at all?

Nope, she says. And then she laughs and James realizes, like, whatever, it's cool to know her, and maybe they'll be MySpace friends or something when she leaves for the bay and he goes home. But the thing he realizes is that he doesn't have to feel fucked up about her talking about gender and how she thinks he should transition and like, Who The Fuck Am I, because he's not trans. Like, maybe, who knows, but he's certainly not transitioning any time soon. He has a girlfriend and a job and even though he's not close with his dad or anything how the fuck do you tell him that shit? So whatever. And when he realizes that he doesn't have to feel all fucked up just because this girl thinks he's trans and wants him to become a woman or whatever, it's like he takes the first deep breath he's taken in twenty-four hours and then he feels kind of serene, almost, sitting at this table. Fucked up on some level, sure, and definitely he wants to smoke again, but he always wants to smoke again.

Sitting in this shitty restaurant eating nachos and pumping quarter after quarter into this video poker machine, listening to Maria monologue about what she thinks they should do in Reno, he's like, whatever. Cool. He's starting to shake this fucked up feeling. It feels good. He's made a decision. He leans back and loses at video poker again. He's like, Who fucking cares that half the graduating class from my high school moved to Reno and they're probably watching me eat nachos with a transsexual right now. He even starts to think, Maybe that is cool.

Okay, Maria asks, So we'll just go find a casino and kick it there and they'll bring us free drinks and we can just hang out?

Yeah, cool, he says.

That's been the plan every time he's been to Reno.

They throw out their hardened cheese and wax paper and tinfoil and James heads for the front door but Maria's like, hold on, I'm going to do a thing. She tosses him the key to the stolen car and walks toward the bathroom and he's kind of like, uh, but then goes outside and gets in the passenger seat. He doesn't really let himself know what's happening but he opens up his messenger bag in his lap and tries to look like he's rooting around in it, like for a wallet or something, but what he's actually doing is opening up the glove box, taking out her sock full of heroin, taking the interior sock out of the exterior sock, unballing the interior sock, and dumping like half of the heroin into his messenger bag. He's not sure exactly what he was expecting. Like, just raw white powder bunched up in a sock seemed possible but unlikely. But it was just these kind of orderly and mundane-looking little wax paper packets and maybe he accidentally took way more than he meant to, but whatever.

They spill into his bag and he rolls the one sock back up, rolls it into the other sock, frantically lunges them back into the glove box, closes it, and zips up his bag. When he looks up he fully expects Maria to be standing over him at the passenger side window with, like, a gun drawn or something, but she's actually nowhere to be seen. He has, like, five minutes or maybe more to wonder whether she saw him stealing her drugs and is doing something horrible. Obviously something other than calling the cops although maybe somebody else called the cops and she knows and she's already three towns over. Maybe the whole thing was a setup! But then she strolls out from around the back of the counter inside the restaurant, obliviously opens the door, and tries the driver door. He hasn't unlocked it. He pushes the automatic unlock button at the same time that she pulls the handle.

This happens three times until Maria takes two steps back from the car, puts her hands above her shoulders, and he manages to unlock the door.

James has covered his tracks superbly, nothing is amiss. He is the greatest criminal that ever lived. Maria points the car toward the tall buildings downtown. Whatever.

28.

It's weird because like even though he's just stolen a bunch of heroin from this girl, which when you put it like that it is definitely the most hardcore thing he's ever done, he's totally cool. Maybe not showing his hand emotionally is, like, his super power. There's no parking downtown and he still hasn't texted Nicole so when they can't find a place to leave the car Maria's like fuck dude, I thought this place was slot machines and free drinks as far as the eye could see and he's like, Well, all the really big casinos with the giant parking lots are a little bit outside of town. Pretty much you just point your shit back toward the highway and you'll bump into one. They're everywhere.

Maria's like, Cool, so they head back outside of town and like five minutes later they're parking in this sprawling parking lot in the shadow of a mountain that's been blasted out to make room for the highway. Well it's not really shady yet, but you can tell that the mountain is to the west of the casino so that when the sun even starts to go down there'll be shade. There are RVs at one end of the parking lot and you can feel the air conditioning blasting out the door of the casino, this huge ultramodern dodecahedron or some complicated shape made of glass they must polish a couple times a day and all these harsh angles. Which is weird, you'd think they'd want a casino to be more inviting but maybe when there are twenty-five epic casinos in your town they can't all have fucking covered wagons and cowboys on them. Maria parks the car and hops out and you can see on her face that she's totally stoked to be here, which is cool, so for a second James gets kind of stoked too but then he's like, I don't really have any money for gambling, and it is depressing as fuck to play penny slots for even half an hour. So. Fuck.

Plus, how is he going to get home? Way to make an exit plan, brilliant strategist. Greatest criminal who ever lived.

29.

She's like Okay, cool, let's lose some fuckin' money.

It's freezing and disorienting inside, which of course it's supposed to be. It's this huge dark cavern where you can't tell what's a wall and what's a mirror. There are lines of garish neon up by the ceiling and tons of old people smoking cigarettes, ashing into the little trays attached to the slot machines and video poker machine and machines that play games James doesn't even know. Right when you walk in there's a little elevated restaurant off to the side with a salad bar full of food that looks plastic and gross but the menu on a stand out front makes it clear that this shit is fancy and James is like, I wonder if I could get away with smoking weed instead of cigarettes while I play penny slots and don't talk to Maria. Then he's like, I wonder if I could get away with doing a bump of heroin in the bathroom. Doubtful. How much goes in a bump? What if he throws up and dies? Obviously at some point he's going to google the mechanics and try it but he kind of doesn't even want to try heroin at all. Whatever.

Maria's already gone. Maybe she already forgot about him. He was a project she thought she could solve, but since he's not doing whatever she wants now he's old news. She's practically saying, out loud, Fuck you, James H., get the fuck out. So he's like, All right. Bye.

You can't tell how deep the casino is. It keeps looking like, okay, here's the wall at the other end, and there's definitely a wall there, but then your eyes follow the wall fifteen feet and there's a corner that opens out onto a whole new collection of green felt tables and people playing actual physical cards. She's gone, dude, James has no fucking idea where Maria is, but looking for her is a project so he goes for it. It's kind of cool to take in a casino and look at the people and stuff, and it's cheaper than buying drinks or pumping quarters into slots. There's this movie that came out ten years before James was born called Joysticks, this stupid eighties teen sex comedy that is pretty much unwatchable, and in the opening scene there's this girl playing Frogger, or Moon Rover, or something, wearing these tiny shorts and this tiny tank top, while the singer wails this song that goes, 'Totally awesome! Video games!' James has an mp3 of that song because it's so fucking dumb that it rules and that's what he's thinking about while he walks around watching people play totally awesome video poker and totally awesome video slots and totally awesome who even knows what. Keno.

Eventually he finds her. Turns out there are a bunch of other entrances but she's not far from the one where they came in, she's just around a corner a little. She's playing a Munsters video slot machine, a quarter at a time.

He's like Hey and she's like Hey and he's like Uh and she's like, did you get a drink? He's like, a buck for a Coke, fuck that, and she's like, Want me to get you a beer? He goes Nah, I think I'm gonna go smoke.

She's like, Cool, and the stupid rockabilly Munsters theme song plays for a couple seconds while the wheels spin again.

James goes outside to find a place to smoke.

Would anybody even care if they caught him smoking weed? Like, bouncers or whatever. Do cops patrol casinos? They must.

He does a whole lap around the casino, which takes a while because it's fucking huge, but there's nothing to hide behind anywhere unless he wants to either climb that mutilated mountain or try to figure out a way around it. He's like, god dammit, this is fucking stupid, what am I doing in Reno with this stranger who doesn't give a fuck about me. He flips out pretty hard for a second and then without even really thinking about it he wanders over to the downtown shuttle and people are getting on so he lines up and gets on too.

30

Nicole comes and picks him up in a couple hours. He lies and doesn't mention Maria or heroin or anything, he says he bumped into Mark this morning and rode into Reno with him, then lost track of him.

Mark isn't answering his texts, James says. I don't know.

Nicole drives him past the gas station where he and Maria pulled over so he could smoke out. The sun's on its way down but it's not really dark out or anything and he's thinking about whether they could pull over at the truckstop outside Star City where they went to on their first date. He wonders whether the yellow light and nostalgia can turn his body inconsequential enough to get hard. He wonders whether there's enough room in the back seat of Nicole's car for her to give him head.

IMOGEN BINNIE

writes a monthly column in *Maximum Rocknroll* magazine, as well as the zines *The Fact That It's Funny Doesn't Make It A Joke* and *Stereotype Threat*. Her work has appeared in *Aorta* magazine, The Skinny, PrettyQueer, and the Topside Press anthology *The Collection: Short Fiction from the Transgender Vanguard*. She lives with her girlfriend and their dog Pants.

Her website is keepyourbridgesburning.com.

OTHER TITLES AVAILABLE NOW from **TOPSIDE PRESS**

THE COLLECTION
Short Fiction from the Transgender Vanguard
edited by *Tom Léger & Riley MacLeod*

A dynamic composite of rising stars, *The Collection* represents the depth and range of tomorrow's finest writers chronicling transgender narratives. 28 authors from North America converge in a single volume to showcase the future of trans literature and the next great movements in queer art.

19.95 paperback • 32.95 hardcover

MY AWESOME PLACE
The Autobiography of Cheryl B
written by *Cheryl Burke*

A rare authentic glimpse into the electrifying arts scene of New York City's East Village during the vibrant 1990s, *My Awesome Place* is the chronicle of a movement through the eyes of one young woman working to cultivate her voice while making peace with her difficult and often abusive family.

An unlikely story for someone whose guidance counselor recommended a career as a toll taker on the New Jersey Turnpike, Burke was determined to escape her circumstances by any means available–physical, intellectual or psychotropic. Her rise to prominence as the spoken word artist known as Cheryl B brought with it a series of destructive girlfriends and boyfriends and a dependence on drugs and alcohol that would take nearly a decade to shake.

15.95 paperback • 25.95 hardcover

UPCOMING RELEASES from **TOPSIDE PRESS**

FREAK OF NURTURE
stories and essays by *Kelli Dunham* • May 2013

Freak of Nurture demonstrates that hilarity and chaos reign when you combine what Kelli's therapist calls "deep biological optimism" with a hearty midwestern work ethic and determination to make bad ideas a fantastic reality. Whether she is writing about hitch-hiking across Haiti to help out with disaster relief or living on a houseboat in Philadelphia in the winter, Kelli Dunham's humorous interpretation of difficult situations is both inspiring and entertaining. In the tradition of authors such as David Sedaris and Ellen DeGeneres, Dunham's "slice of life" stories remind us that even though humans are deeply flawed, we're also seriously hysterical that way.

READY, AMY, FIRE
a novel by *Red Durkin* • Summer 2013

Hans Tronsmon is an average 20 year-old transgender man. He's the popular chair of the transmasculine caucus at his women's college and the first draft of his memoir is almost finished. But his world is turned upside down when his happily married gay dads decide to stop paying for his off-campus apartment and start saving for retirement. Hans must learn to navigate the world of part-time jobs, publishing, and packers if he wants to survive. *Ready, Amy, Fire* is the harrowing tale of one man's courageous journey into boyhood.

MORE INFO: WWW.TOPSIDEPRESS.COM

Made in the USA
Lexington, KY
30 June 2014